QUESTIONING HEAVEN

Adapted from
William Shakespeare's
King Lear

by
Ching-Hsi Perng and Fang Chen
Translated by Ching-Hsi Perng

STUDENT BOOK CO., LTD.

QUESTIONING HEAVEN
by Ching-Hsi Perng and Fang Chen
English Translation by Ching-Hsi Perng

No.11, Lane 75, Sec. 1, He-Ping E. Rd., Taipei, Taiwan
http://www.studentbook.com.tw
email: student.book@msa.hinet.net

ISBN 978-957-15-1687-5

Preface: "Song of Despair"

Joseph Graves[*]
Artistic Director, Institute of World Theatre and Film

Peking University

Garcia Lorca ends his play *Blood Wedding* with the words, "*la oscura raiz del grito*"—"the dark root of the scream". The image suggests better than abstract language where Shakespeare takes us with *King Lear*. The scream begins where words and endurance end. Along the same lines, Pascal says at one point, roughly translated, "The eternal silence of all those infinite spaces terrifies me." Pascal is our greatest tragic thinker: an intellectual concept has put him in an intellectual panic; Shakespeare takes us a step further. He gives us in *King Lear* tragic poetry where, certainly, the intellectual element has not been eliminated, but rather fused with the sensuous. Shakespeare rooted the intellectual elements of his play in the sensuousness of its characters, as indeed God seems to have done when He made each one of us. The intellect can acknowledge the eternal mystery of tragic

---

[*] Joseph Graves is a playwright, director, and actor. His works have been seen in numerous countries, including the United States, Great Britain, France, Italy, Russia, New Zealand, Taiwan, and throughout the Middle East and China.

things, can be afraid of them, but only the body can experience the full feel of tragedy, can find the intellectual fear transformed into soul-shaking awe at the inexplicable, and, consequently, scream.

Ching-Hsi Perng and Fang Chen set for themselves the monumental task of translating into Chinese words Shakespeare's English words of *King Lear* (a thoroughly challenging undertaking on its own), then added enormously to that considerable challenge by seeking to use the elements of indigenous cultural sensuousness found in Bangzi Opera to capture the totality of the tragic poetry of *King Lear* in their adaptation of that play, *Questioning Heaven.*

They succeeded splendidly on every level in their magnificent work and our Chinese audiences and readers will, no doubt, benefit from their literary, poetic and theatrical creation for years to come. Their ability to catch the full scope of *King Lear*'s story while keeping their own adaptation to manageable playing length is remarkable. In particular, the blending of many of *King Lear*'s scenes into a few near their play's closing motions is not only wonderfully clever, but powerfully effective. It is the work of two skilled and diligent translators who are also true artists in their own right.

Pierre-Amie Touchard has a splendidly simple phrase for the phenomenon tragedy. He calls it a "song of despair." I have always thought that phrase an exquisite paradox because tragedy does not sing. If a despairing man starts to sing he is already transcending the despair. His song is the transcendence. But Ching-Hsi and Fang have made me readjust my thoughts regarding Touchard's phrase, for their adaptation of *King Lear* is a glorious song of despair in which literal singing is very much part and parcel of the deeply moving tragic poetry.

I am grateful to Ching-Hsi Perng and Fang Chen for their thrillingly unique and beautifully magical adaptation/creation, *Questioning Heaven.*

Translator's Note:

Once again, it is with great pleasure and most sincere gratitude
that I record here my indebtedness to
two most admirable friends—
Tom Sellari, Poet, Shakespearean scholar, and Professor
at National Chengchi University, Taiwan,
and
Joseph Graves, accomplished Actor, Director, Playwright,
and
Artistic Director of Peking University's
Institute of World Theatre and Film.
They read an earlier version of the translation
with loving care and critical acumen
and offered a wealth of useful suggestions for improvement,
most of which have been incorporated here.
Any infelicities that remain are of course
solely my responsibility.
Special thanks go to Joe,
whose succinct and insightful preface
graces this adaptation.

Questioning Heaven, premiered on 27 November 2015 at National Theatre, Taipei, Taiwan, was produced by Taiwan Bangzi Company.

Director	PO-SHEN LU
Technical Director	CHING-CHUN YIN
Bin Hela (Empress)	HAI-LING WANG
Du Xu (Xu)	YANG-LING HSIAO
Du Shao (Shao)	HSUAN-TING CHANG
Du Wei (Wei)	WEN-CHI HSIEH
Duanmu Ge (Duanmu)	HAI-SHAN CHU
Duanmu Jia (A-Jia)	YI-SHENG CHANG
Duanmu Meng (A-Meng)	CHIAN-HUA LIU
Situ De (Situ)	CHING-CHUN YIN
You Dan (Fool)	YANG-WEI CHENG
Nangong Ao (Nangong)	HUI-CHEN LIEN
Xiahou Kang (Xiahou)	CHANG-MIN HU
King of Helian (Helian)	WEN-WEI LIN
Lord of Xianyu (Xianyu)	YUAN-MAO LIN
Shangguan Feng (Shangguan)	CHUAN-HAO TU
Guards/Attendants	YU-MAO CHANG,
	CHIH-HUNG LEE,
	YUAN-CHING YANG,
	WEN-WEI LIN,

	YUAN-MAO LIN,
	YANG-CHEN HSIAO
Dancers	YANG-LAN CHANG,
	YI-TING SUN,
	YEN-JU CHEN,
	YUAN-LIANG KUO,
	HAI-LIEN TENG
Composer	TING-YING ZHANG
Music Arrangement	JIN-CHI CHEN
Costume Design	YU-SHEN LI
Stage Design	PO-LIN LI
Light Design	LISA HSU
Image Design	YI-SHENG WANG

Table of Contents

List of Characters

BIN HELA	Emperess of Xuanyuan (**EMPRESS**)
DU XU	Bin Hela's eldest daughter (**XU**)
DU SHAO	Bin Hela's second daughter (**SHAO**)
DU WEI	Bin Hela's youngest daughter (**WEI**)
DUANMU GE	Senior Minister of Xuanyuan (**DUANMU**)
DUANMU JIA	Duanmu Ge's son and legitimate heir, later disguised as a mad monk (**A-JIA**)
DUANMU MENG	Duanmu Ge's bastard son (**A-MENG**)
SITU DE	Loyal minister of Xuanyuan, later disguised as Gongsun Kai (**SITU**)
YOU DAN	Clown to the Empress (**FOOL**)
NANGONG AO	Du Xu's husband (**NANGONG**)
XIAHOU KANG	Du Shao's husband (**XIAHOU**)
KING OF HELIAN	A suitor to Du Wei, later her husband (**HELIAN**)
LORD OF XIANYU	A suitor to Du Wei (**XIANYU**)
SHANGGUAN FENG	Steward of Du Xu's household (**SHANGGUAN**)
1ST GUARD	Under the Empress
2ND GUARD	Under Xiahou
3RD GUARD	Under Nangong

CAPTAIN   Under Duanmu Meng

A number of guards, under the Empress, Nangong, Xhiahou, Duanmu,
     and Helian, respectively, to be distinguished by their uniforms

Several lords

Some soldiers / guards

List of Scenes

Prologue

(Location: The palace of Xuanyuan)

(GUARDS, LORDS, SITU DE, DUANMU GE, NANGONG NANGONG *and* DU XU, XIAHOU *and* DU SHAO, *and* DU WEI *take their places before* EMPRESS BIN HELA, *in elegant dress and imperious, slowly walks in. Songs and dances precede the feast.*)

>[Chorus, *offstage*]:
>> **Ten thousand flowers bring in warmth of spring;**
>> **Loud drums and cymbals reach the heavens' gate.**
>> **In Hall of Lasting Peace the royals sing.**
>> **May bliss of Xuanyuan Empress ne'er abate!**
>
>[Solo, *offstage*]:
>> **Her Majesty Supreme has now ordained**
>> **This day her land in three parts to divide.**
>
>[Chorus, *offstage*]:
>> **The court entire in silence holds their breath,**
>> **All wond'ring just what she will decide.**

(*Carried on to* Scene One.)

Scene 1: Marketing Love

ALL: (*as they bow*) Most happy birthday to your majesty! Endless be your felicity!

EMPRESS: Ha, Ha! At ease.

> (*sings*)
>
> **Full eighteen springs have gone since I did gain**
> **This lonely throne to rule this land alone.**
> **Unceasing wars have aged me, worn me down;**
> **For always all details I oversaw.**
> **And now, at last, the land is unified;**
> **It's time for me to rest in dignity,**
> **To ancestors and heaven sacrifice,**
> **And Xuanyuan Empire cut in three.**
>
> (*All nod in agreement.*)

DUANMU: Your Majesty proclaimed this not long ago. We all await your judicious decision.

EMPRESS: Very well.

> (*to* DUANMU) My Lord Duanmu, the ceremony is complete. Go and invite the King of Helian and the Lord of Xianyu to the feast.

DUANMU: I shall, your majesty. (*exit*)

EMPRESS: Fetch me the map.

(*One* GUARD *presents the map.*)

EMPRESS: You all know that early on, when his majesty was ill, I
had to take care of state affairs on his behalf. Then he
passed away, leaving behind just three tender daughters.
With threats both home and abroad, I had to ascend the
throne to safeguard the land. Thanks to your assistance,
together we fought north and south, everyone braving
death—hence the peace we enjoy today. On this auspicious
day I would like to make an important announcement.

(*sings*)

> **Essential it is that the royal line continues,**
>
> **And the state prospers for generations on end.**

(*pauses, surveying the court*)

> **You loving daughters mine, now tell the world**
>
> **How much you love me, and I shall allot**
>
> **My land based on expressions of that love,**
>
> **Impartial, in my own love to you all.**

ALL: (*greatly taken by surprise, they look at each other, murmuring*)
What's this? What's this? By words? Get the land by
flattering words?

(EMPRESS *winks at* 1 ST GUARD, *and he steps forward.*)

1 ST GUARD: (*loudly*) Quiet! (*steps back*)

(*Quietly everyone looks at* EMPRESS.)

EMPRESS: You all have heard. It is my wish to leave state affairs to the three princesses so that I can enjoy my twilight age. The more filial shall have the more grace. Nangong and Xiahou, as consort princes, shall also help rule the land.

NANGONG and XIAHOU: (*look at each other, and then*) Yes, your majesty.

EMPRESS: You, dear Xu, our eldest daughter, speak first. Let us know your love.

XU: (*steps forward with a huge smile*) Your sagacious majesty—

(*pondering as she sings*)

> **You've been to me a grand, sheltering tree:**
> **A willow mother and an oak-like father.**

(*after a slight pause*)

> **I know no other treasure save my mom,**
> **The leafy jewel of Xuanyuan—you.**
> **No words can ever describe**
> **My true love for your majesty, my mother.**

(*her eyes rolling*)

> **I'll ever tend your health and happiness—**

EMPRESS: (*satisfied, interrupts*) Well, well, well.

XU: (*continues to sing*)

> **Forever by your side: I'll never leave.**

SHAO: (*aside*) Aiya! What a fawner! But I can outdo you!

WEI: (*aside*) What shall I say? A clear conscience can never utter such exaggeration.

EMPRESS: (*pointing at the map*) From the northwest to the
northeast, the entire stretch of rich hills, river, and
extensive plain we give to you and Nangong.

XU and NANGONG: We humbly thank your majesty.

EMPRESS: Now it's your turn, dear Shao. Speak.

SHAO: (*glances at* XU, *then with a flattering smile*) My dearest
mother, your majesty—

(*sings*)

> **Made of the same mettle as my sister, I**
> **Sincerely speak and what I say is true.**
> **I love you, mother, more than my own life,**
> **For every thought of mine goes straight to you.**
> **Together shall we watch sweet scenes by day;**
> **At night in the Hall of Bliss songs of heaven hear.**
> **And if the Eastern winds would but assist,**
> **I'd even catch the moon and stars for you.**

WEI: (*aside*) Ah, merciful heaven! The gods alone can know my
filial love.

EMPRESS: Ha, ha! To you and Xiahou, and your offspring,
(*pointing at the map*) one third of this great land, forever.
The southwestern part is no less in value than that
conferred to your elder sister.

SHAO and XIAHOU: We humbly thank your majesty for your
abundant grace.

EMPRESS: Now, (*to* WEI, *in a much more gentle tone*) our joy,
posthumously born, who never got to see your father, I
have been negligent in caring for you, but for you I have
kept the fairest share. Either King of Helian or Lord of
Xianyu, when he becomes consort prince, will share this
dowry with you. Come now, speak. I'm waiting.

WEI: I . . . . Nothing, your majesty.

(*All are surprised.*)

EMPRESS: (*astonished*) Nothing?

WEI: Nothing.

EMPRESS: Nothing will come of nothing. Speak again.

WEI: Unhappy that I am, I have no flowery words but love you with
my conscience.

EMPRESS: How, how, dear Wei? Mend your speech, lest you may
mar the fortunes I've prepared for you.

WEI: Your majesty—

(*sings*)

> **Parental love and care are boundless things—**
> **This has not changed from first and never will.**
> **To give you back such kindness as you gave**
> **To me and to my sisters, that's my hope;**
> **But word's false eloquence I must eschew,**
> **Or risk my feelings real, you misconstrue.**

EMPRESS: Does your heart go with this?

WEI: Yes. (*continues to sing*)

> **I humbly beg your majesty to see**
>
> **In naturalness are truthful feelings found.**

EMPRESS: So young and so untender?

WEI: So young, your majesty, and true.

EMPRESS: (*furious*) Humph! You—you—

> (*sings an aside*)
>
> **Your words unsaid, and spoken, make me rage!**
>
> **Oh, willful, thankless thing, you do defy**
>
> **In open court with total disregard**
>
> **For majesty, and mock our dignity.**

> (*speaks*) Well, let it be so. Your truth then be your dower.

> (*continues to sing*)
>
> **Here we disclaim all our maternal care;**
>
> **By sacred earth and heaven I do swear.**

> (*Shocked, the entire court is silent for a moment.*)

SITU: Good my liege—

EMPRESS: Peace, Situ!

> (*continues to sing*)
>
> **Ridiculous that I with wishful thought**
>
> **Would plan to rest on her kind nursery.**

> (*to* WEI, *speaks*) Out! Out of my sight! You're no daughter of mine! (WEI *backs a few steps.*)

> (*to the* GUARDS) Call Lord Xianyu. Stir! Call King of

Helian. (*Exit two* GUARDS.)

(*to* NANGONG *and* XIAHOU, *speaks*) You consort princes: besides the dowry bestowed to the two princesses, (*pointing to the map*) you shall share equally that large portion of land there. From now on, Xuanyuan will be ruled by your two houses.

NANGONG and XIAHOU: Yes, your majesty.

EMPRESS: But we shall retain a sovereign's title, and all the additions to it. Ourself, with a hundred knights, shall in turns make our abode with you.

(*takes out the royal seal*) Come, for confirmation we bestow to you this royal seal.

(NANGONG *and* XIAHOU *step forward to accept it.*)

SITU: Your majesty, I have always been obedient to you and never run counter . . .

EMPRESS: My mind is made up. No more words.

SITU: Pardon me, my liege. Even when the sun is eclipsed by clouds and villains hold sway, your servant shall speak the truth. Revoke your command. I dare answer with my life that Princess Wei does not love you least. Ineloquence does not mean lack of filial affection.

EMPRESS: Situ! On your life, no more!

SITU: Your loyal servant, I've never feared to lose my life for you.

EMPRESS: Out of my sight!

SITU: Your majesty shall regret it.

EMPRESS: O miscreant! Take him away and chop off his head!

> (*general panic in the court*)

NANGONG and WEI: Dear liege, forbear!

SITU: Think twice, your majesty.

EMPRESS: (*furious*) Ah, so you think you're a loyal minister and dare to admonish us. Well now, go make provision and get out of Xuanyuan. If after three days you're found in our dominion, that moment is your death. Away!

SITU: Well, then, a minister can only discharge his duty when the sovereign acts like one. Banishment is perhaps better. Fare you well, my liege.

> (*to* WEI) Take care, Princess.

WEI: (*with reluctance*) My lord Situ!

SITU: (*to* XU *and* SHAO) May your deeds approve your speeches.

> (XU *and* SHAO *return his words with cold stares.*)
>
> (*looks around*) I bid you all farewell. (*Exit.*)
>
> (*Enter a* GUARD.)

GUARD: Your majesty, King of Helian and Lord of Xianyu are here.

> (*Enter* HELIAN, XIANYU, *and* DUANMU.)

HELIAN, XIANYU, and DUANMU: (*bowing to* EMPRESS) Most royal majesty.

EMPRESS: At ease.

> (DUANMU *returns to his place.*)

My lords, you've come in quest of my youngest daughter's hand, and I did intend to give her a handsome dowry. But now her price has fallen deep. There (*glances at* WEI) she stands.

(*to* LORD OF XIANYU) My lord, we first address to you: Will you take her?

XIANYU: (*confused*) Your majesty, I crave no more than what your highness offered.

EMPRESS: She is no longer our dear daughter. Not only is she dower-less, but she is pieced with our displeasure. If this pleases you, take her away.

XIANYU: Ah? Well . . . (*takes a look at* WEI) I know no answer.

EMPRESS: This heartless creature, newly adopted to our hate, is dowered with our curse. Will you take her or leave her?

XIANYU: If so, well then . . . (*lowering his head*) she is too precious for me.

WEI: (*aside*) Nor would I debase myself and marry one whose love is wealth and power.

EMPRESS: (*to* KING OF HELIAN) Dear Sir, since our former emperor was a sworn brother to your father, we are reluctant to match you where we hate. Therefore I beseech you to find someone more worthy.

HELIAN: This is most strange. Has she who even now was your dearest daughter, the apple of your eye, committed some monstrous crime in a trice of time? What unnatural offence both to gods and reason has she done?

WEI: (*steps forward*) I yet beseech your majesty to make clear that it is my lack of that glib and oily art of flattery, not any shameless behavior or unchaste action, that has deprived me of your grace and favor.

EMPRESS: Go to, better you had not been born than not to have pleased me better, you hussy!

HELIAN: Is it no more but this? A tardiness in nature that cannot flatter? Look at this beautiful princess—

(*sings*)

> **By nature pure and fresh,**
>
> **As clean as lotus white.**
>
> **Such beauty modest is**
>
> **Delicate and loving.**
>
> **Her eyes show treatment wrong;**
>
> **Her bearing owns my heart.**

(*walks up to her to take her hand, then continues singing*)

> **Like lovebirds twain shall we return**
>
> **As king and queen to our fair Helian.**

(*turns to* EMPRESS) Your majesty, be it lawful I take up what's cast away. I am willing to marry the princess.

EMPRESS: Huh? As I have said, she has no dowry. Nothing.

HELIAN: "A lady full of grace is the right mate for a gentleman."—

She is herself dowry enough. If she is not welcome here,
she will be our queen, to rule over Helian with us.

EMPRESS: Well, you have her. We have no such daughter, nor
shall ever see that face of hers again. Therefore, be gone.

HELIAN: (*to* WEI) Bid farewell to them, Princess.

(WEI *steps forward in an attempt to take leave of*
EMPRESS, *who walks away in anger, followed by the*
retinue. DUANMU *opens his mouth to speak, stops himself,*
saying nothing as he exits. XU *and* SHAO *remain onstage.*)
(HELIAN *steps forward to comfort* WEI) Do not take their
unkindness to heart. You have lost here, a better where to
find.

WEI: (*to her sisters*) Dear sisters, love well our mother.

XU: Prescribe not our duty.

SHAO: Just mind your own business.

WEI: I . . .

(*Shaking his head,* KING OF HELIAN *takes up* WEI'S
hand as they exit.)

XU: (*aside*) Ya, this—

(*sings an aside*)

What joy this brings—this radical change!

Without my stirring, half an empire's gained.

SHAO: (*continues the aside in song*)

With favor lost, our sister Wei is cast off:

Most unreasonably did Mother behave.

XU: Sister, I think mother will leave tonight.

SHAO: That's most certain, and with you. Next month with us.

XU: You see how full of changes she is! (*steps forward to hold* SHAO*'s hand and taps it gently*) Such inconstant starts are we likely to have from her.

SHAO: Exactly. Sooner or later we'll be the victims.

XU: We have to do something.

SHAO: And quickly too.

XU: (*continues the aside in song*)

Such fits of rage portend some future ills;

SHAO: (*continues the aside in song*)

Care must be taken with erratic queens.

XU: (*continues the aside in song*)

What does our future hold—

A fortune good or bad?

SHAO: (*continues the aside in song*)

Half worry and half bliss—

XU and SHAO: (*sing together*)

Oh, how can we rejoice?

(*Light dims.*)

Scene 2: Incitement

(Location: Duanmu's mansion)

(*Enter* A-MENG, *reading from a letter, very pleased with himself.*)
A-MENG: (*declaims*)

> "Old thief get more tyrannical with age;
> Preposterous to so revere the old.
> In vain we do their tyranny endure,
> Till we're too old inheritance to love.
> No wishful thinking 'tis to share his riches now:
> To shove him on to heaven's all we need.
> Long hesitation brings us nothing close—
> We'll in some secret conversation talk."

(*sings*)

> Fame and fortune are not endowed at birth;
> You must with craftiness, deception, steal.
> Why should the younger be to baseness cast?
> The bastard has a way to power seize.

(*Enter* DUANMU *from the other direction.*)

(*seeing* DUANMU) Ha, here comes the old man.

DUANMU: (*talking to himself*) Situ banished? The King of Helian rushed home? And the empress gone last night? Gave up her power to live under someone else's roof? All this

happened so unexpectedly!

(*seeing* A-MENG) How now, A-Meng, what news?

A-MENG: Er, sir, nothing. None. (*quickly pockets the letter*)

DUANMU: Why such a flurry of hands?

A-MENG: Well . . . nothing—nothing, sir.

DUANMU: What letter were you reading?

A-MENG: Nothing, sir.

DUANMU: Nothing? Why then did you try to hide it? Come, let's

see it.

A-MENG: I beseech you, sir, pardon me. It is a letter from my

brother. I find it unfit for your reading.

DUANMU: Give me the letter!

A-MENG: I beg your pardon, sir. You mustn't read this.

DUANMU: Give it me! Your father will see it.

(A-MENG *retrieves the letter, which* DUANMU *snatches.*)

A-MENG: I hope brother wrote it only to test me.

DUANMU: (*reads; astonished*) "Old thieves get more tyrannical

with age; Preposterous to so revere the old. . . ." Ha! what

can this mean?—

(*sings*)

> **Since the creation of the world, the rule**
> **Has been to venerate the old and good.**
> **What does the saucy boy complain about?**

"Old thief" he calls me, for crying out loud!

(*speaks*) When did you get this? Who brought it?

A-MENG: It wasn't brought me, Sir. I found it in my bedroom early in the morning.

DUANMU: Do you recognize the handwriting? Is it your brother's?

A-MENG: If the content were good, sir, I'd swear it's his. But as it is, I—I dare not say so.

DUANMU: (*examines the writing*) It is A-Jia's handwriting.

(*reads on, sings on*)

To rob me early of my property,

He'd send me now into the underworld?

(*speaks*) A-Jia? How could he write such a letter? How could he entertain such a thought? O villain, villain! Abhorred villain! Unnatural, brutish beast! No, worse than brutish beasts!

A-MENG: Sir, maybe he was just joking. He couldn't be serious.

DUANMU: (*reads on, sings on*)

So greedy and so cunning, can he be?

Unfit to crawl between the earth and sky!

(*speaks*) Go, A-Meng, find him out. Hang him I will. Where could this heartless villain be?

A-MENG: I don't know, sir. Please suspend your wrath till the truth be known. He may have written this to feel out my affection for you.

DUANMU: You think so?

A-MENG: Allow me, sir, to make arrangement for you to listen to
what he says.

DUANMU: (*shaking his head*) He cannot be such a monster. A-
Meng, seek him out. Take action as you see fit. I must get
to the bottom of this.

A-MENG: Yes, my lord.

DUANMU: Ah, the astrological phenomena lately—

(*sings*)

> **Strange sun, strange moon do both the birds alarm;**
> **It's springtime yet the plants all shrivel up.**
> **What happens, good or bad? 'tis Nature does**
> **Presage the human world, and we are doomed.**
> **Love cools between the parent and the child.**
> **Bonds crack. Behind, ahead, I see in fear.**

(*speaks*) A-Meng, find out this villain. Do it carefully.

A-MENG: I'll do it immediately. Please rest and wait for my news.

DUANMU: All right. (*Exits.*)

A-MENG: Brainless old man! What a fool! When we deserve ill
fortune, we blame it on planetary influence. "Nature does
presage the human world"!—Fie! An admirable evasion!
(*Enter A-JIA.*)
Pat he comes.

A-JIA: How now, A-Meng, what serious contemplation are you in?

A-MENG: Brother, I've been studying divination, in connection with
       eclipses of sun and moon.

A-JIA: (*disapprovingly*) Do you busy yourself with that?

A-MENG: Why not? The prophecies have all come true.
       When did you see our father last?

A-JIA: Why, last night.

A-MENG: Did you speak with him?

A-JIA: Yeah, for about an hour.

A-MENG: How did you part? Was he not angry at you?

A-JIA: No, not at all.

A-MENG: Think again where you've offended Father. At this
      moment he's so enraged that even killing you would
      scarcely pacify him. I suggest that you stay away from him
      for now.

A-JIA: Ah? Is this true? Then some villain must have done me
      wrong.

A-MENG: I thought so too. Now retire to my bedroom. When he
      cools down, I'll bring you to him. Away now! (A-JIA
      hesitates) Go!
      (*Exit* A-JIA *in a hurry.*)

A-MENG: Humph! Why should the fools in the court call me base, a
      base bastard? My body is excellently formed, my features
      very handsome, and I'm shaped like my father. Why then
      do they brand me with bastardy? That term I defy!

Humph!—

(*sings*)

> **I lie through my sharp teeth to take them in,**
> **Inventions clever to turn them into foes.**
> **A-Jia helps with his foolish honesty,**
> **And father, with his huge credulity.**

(*speaks*) Just wait and see, A-Jia! A-Meng shall grow and prosper, and top the "legitimate" fool! (*keeps snickering*) Hah, hah, hah . . .

(*Light dims.*)

Scene 3: Insulting the Parent

(Location: Outside of Du Xu's Palace)

(*The Empress' GUARDS, in groups, perform shows to raucous music: some swallow knives and spit fire; some change masks and somersault; some haul cauldrons or climb up long poles; some dance or duel.*)

(*Enter* EMPRESS *with several rowdy* GUARDS *frolicking and hitting drums.*)

> [Chorus, *offstage*]:
>
> **The shadows dance to music wild and loud;**
> **And say such celebration honor peace.**
> **The soldiers brave have grown so tired of war,**
> **Like gods they spend their time thus, wontonly.**

EMPRESS: (*continues to sing*)

> **While we make merry secret night descends**
> **While reveling, who cares if hairs are gray?**
> **Now is the time to best fulfill one's wish:**
> **With abdication but contentment comes.**

GUARDS: (*yelling*) We're starved! Can't wait another jot for dinner!

EMPRESS: (*dismounts*) I'm hungry too. Go, have them get it ready.

> (*Exit an* ATTENDANT.)

(*Enter* SITU *disguised as* GONGSUN KAI.)

SITU: (*smooths his cap and beard, strikes a pose*) Now, banished Situ, you are disguised as Gongsun Kai. By borrowing other accents to disguise your speech, you can continue service in the land of Xuanyuan.

(SITU *comes before* EMPRESS.)

EMPRESS: How now, what are you?

SITU: A very honest fellow, your highness.

EMPRESS: What do you do?

SITU: I can do anything.

EMPRESS: What do you want?

SITU: Service. I want to serve you. For you carry an authority that commands respect. I can run errands, do chores, deliver messages for you—just so I can feed my mouth.

EMPRESS: Ha, ha! You certainly can talk. Follow me, then, to dinner first.

(*leads the* ATTENDANTS *into the palace; shouts*) Let's have dinner! Where's my fool? Go you and call him there.

(*Exit an* ATTENDANT.)

(*Enter* SHANGGUAN, *who crosses the stage.*)

You, you, sirrah, where's my daughter?

SHANGGUAN: (*keeps going without turning his head*) Humph, so please you—

EMPRESS: What does that mumbling fool say? Call the blockhead back.

(*Exit* 1ST GUARD.)

Why is my fool not come yet? Where is everybody?

(*Enter* 1ST GUARD.)

How now, where's that mongrel?

1ST GUARD: He says, your highness, he's too busy.

EMPRESS: He's too busy?

1ST GUARD: Your majesty, I know not why, but these servants seem to serve with less affection than before. There's a great abatement of kindness even in your daughter and the consort prince.

EMPRESS: Ha? Say you so?

1ST GUARD: Pardon me, but my duty cannot be silent when I think your highness wronged.

EMPRESS: Now that you mention it, I have also perceived some neglect of late, which I thought was my oversensitivity. From now on, watch more carefully for us. But where's my fool? I have not seen him these two days.

1ST GUARD: Your majesty, since my young lady's gone to Helian, the fool has much pined away.

EMPRESS: No more of that. I have noted it well. Go and tell my daughter I would speak with her. (*Exit* 1ST GUARD.) You, go and call hither my fool.

(*Exit an* ATTENDANT.)

(*Re-enter* SHANGGUAN.)

EMPRESS: Hey, you, sir. Come over here, sir. (SHANGGUAN *makes faces, neglecting* EMPRESS. SITU *steps up and drags him over.*) Who am I, sir?

SHANGGUAN: (*coldly*) My lady's old queen mother.

EMPRESS: "My lady's old queen mother"? You slave, you cur!

SHANGGUAN: I am not.

EMPRESS: Do you bandy looks with me, you rascal? (*Boxes him on the ear.*)

SHANGGUAN: I'll not be struck.

SITU: Nor tripped neither (*trips him*), you trash.

(SHANGGUAN *struggles to his feet, and is pushed out by* SITU.)

EMPRESS: Well done. You're hired. There's a gold coin for you.

(*gives it to him*)

(*Enter* FOOL.)

FOOL: Give me a gold coin too, Auntie. I can teach you some common sense. Mark—

(*recites to clappers*)

> **Have more than you show.**
> **Know more than you talk.**
> **Lend less than you own.**
> **Ride more than you walk.**
> **Be cautious with dice.**

> **Trust not easily.**
>
> **Leave drinking, whoring, but stay home,**
>
> **Good fortunes you'll see.**

SITU: This is nothing, fool.

FOOL: Isn't it? Rather like the politician's breath—there's nothing in it.

(*to* EMPRESS) Can you make use of nothing?

EMPRESS: Why, no, fool. Nothing can come of nothing.

FOOL: (*to* SITU) Please tell her then, that that is all she has now.

She will not believe a fool.

EMPRESS: A bitter fool!

FOOL: Please, auntie, hire someone to teach me how to lie. I would like to learn to lie.

EMPRESS: If you lie, sirrah, we'll have you whipped.

FOOL: Alas, auntie, I get whipped whether I lie or not. Look here

(*shows his elbow*), even when I hold my tongue, your

daughter would have me whipped. It's tough to be a fool.

And yet I would not be you: you are more fool than I.

(*Enter Princess* XU.)

EMPRESS: How now, daughter, why are you frowning again?

FOOL: When you had no need to care for her frowning, you were

somebody. Now you are an O . . . (*looks at the princess*)

Well, I'll hold my tongue.

(*sings a ditty*)

Mum, mum,

Keep your crust and crumb.

Pretend not to see,

Or (*points to* EMPRESS) **an imbecile be.**

XU: Sir, not only this, your all-licensed fool, but your hundred
knights are insolent. They do hourly carp and quarrel. Yet
you condone them. This is unbearable. Now, to keep the
peace and order of the palace, they must be punished.

FOOL: Don't you know, auntie,

The bush-sparrow fed the cuckoo so long

That it had its head bit off by its young.

EMPRESS: Are you my daughter?

XU: Please make use of your wisdom instead of your temper. You've
been transported of late from what you ought to be.

FOOL: Ha! May not an ass know when the cart draws the horse?

EMPRESS: Does any here know me? Are we not Empress of
Xuanyuan? Are we to be constrained by you?

FOOL: 'Tis worse to have a hollow title than not to have the title at
all.

EMPRESS: Your name, fair lady?

XU: Please, your majesty, stop this pretending! Remember who you
are. As you are old, you should be wise and dignified. You
have no need of one hundred guards in the palace. Please
reduce your train, or else I'll have to do it for you.

EMPRESS: (*shouts*) Saddle my horse, saddle my horse! Call my
    train together.

    (*to* XU) Degenerate bastard, I'll not trouble you. I have yet
    a daughter left.

XU: (*coldly looking at the* GUARDS) Lawless rioters!

EMPRESS: Woe that too late repents! How—how ugly do you show
    compared with your sister Wei!

    Ah! (*beats her own head*) O Bin Hela, Bin Hela, Bin Hela,
    how could you have let your folly in and your judgment out?
    (*sings*)

> **The country faltered when my husband died ,**
> **I shouldered all the chaos all alone.**
> **The baby cried from nightmares through each**
> > **night;**
>
> **I held her weeping till the morning sun.**

XU: Oh my! Why bring up ancient history?

EMPRESS: (*continues singing*)

> **There was a time when I all orders gave;**
> **All nations sang my praise—held me in awe.**
> **Who'd think that this ungrateful daughter should**
> **Care nothing about blood-relationship.**

XU: Your majesty exaggerates.

EMPRESS: (*continues singing*)

> **The crafty little bitch is like a wolf,**

> **While I in anger tremble, full of tears.**

XU: Calm down, ma'am.

EMPRESS: (*continues singing*)

> **I call down retribution from the gods,**
>
> **To cut the lying line of Nangong's house.**

XU: Fie, fie, fie! What nonsense!

EMPRESS: I have another daughter. She will certainly love me and despise you. Humph! Just wait and see. (*Exits in wrath.*)

FOOL: Wait for me, auntie!

> (FOOL, SITU, *and the* GUARDS *run after* EMPRESS.)

XU: Crazy old woman! Do as you wish.

> (*Re-enter* SHANGGUAN.)

XU: How now, have you written the letter to my sister?

SHANGGUAN: Yes, your highness.

XU: Away to horse this instant. This important business of mine can't be delayed.

SHANGGUAN: Yes, your highness. (*rushes off*)

> (*Enter* NANGONG.)

NANGONG: (*looking back*) How very strange!

> (*to* XU) My lady, I just ran into her majesty, and was about to greet her. But she simply ignored me and left in great anger. What's the matter?

XU: Oh, nothing serious. Never mind.

NANGONG: Your highness, even though her majesty has abdicated,

she is still the queen mother. It is only proper that we give
her due respect.

Xu: Humph, I know what I know. You need not lecture me.

NANGONG: Well . . .

Xu: (*aside*) Let me see how much longer your waywardness can last,
humph!

(*Light dims.*)

Scene 4: The Trap

(Location: Duammu's mansion)

(*Enter* A-MENG, *leisurely.*)

A-MENG: The two princesses and Xiahou the consort prince are
coming here this evening? (*his eyes rolling*) Ha! Perfect
timing. This play of mine happens to lack two actors.
(*shouts toward the second floor*) Brother, a word; descend
this instant.
(A-JIA *appears, descends, is greeted by* A-MENG.)
Prince Xiahou has received intelligence that you're plotting
a rebellion. He is rushing this way.

A-JIA: (*shocked*) That's ridiculous! There's no such thing!

A-MENG: Father is watching you. O brother, fly this place!
Ah, Dad is coming. Pardon me, I must pretend. (*he draws
his sword*) Draw! Seem to defend yourself in earnest. (A-
JIA *draws*) Right, that's more like it. (*they fight with each
other; loudly*) Yield, come before Father!—Light ho,
here!—(*whispers to* A-JIA) Fly, brother, eastward.—
(*loudly*) Torches, torches! (*whispers to* A-JIA) Well, take
care. (*Exit* A-JIA.)
(*mumbling*) Some blood drawn on me (*cuts his arm*) would

better convince them.—(*loudly*) Father, father!—Stop, stop! Help!

(*Enter* DUANMU *and* GUARDS *in a rush, carrying torches.*)

DUANMU: A-Meng, are you all right? Where's the villain?

A-MENG: Look, sir, I'm wounded. He hid in the dark and wounded me.

DUANMU: Damn it! Where is he? How serious is your wound?

A-MENG: Not too serious. But you, sir, should be careful, for he intends to kill you.

DUANMU: Where is he?

A-MENG: He fled to the west.

DUANMU: Go after him!

(GUARDS *rush off.*)

A-MENG: Father, when I refused to join him and chastised him for being heartless, he cut me on my defenseless arm.

DUANMU: Humph, unnatural beast! I'll report to the princess and the duke this evening, and proclaim a warrant for his death. Once found, he shall be decapitated on the spot.

A-MENG: Sir, I tried hard to dissuade him from his intent, but he persisted in it. He even had the nerve to say that he doesn't fear being exposed, for I am but a bastard, and nobody would believe me.

DUANMU: O damnable villain! Would he deny his crime? My good son, I'll make sure you inherit my title and revenue.

(*Enter a* GUARD.)

GUARD: Your highness, the princess and the duke are arrived.

DUANMU: Go greet them, quick!

(*Enter* XIAHOU *and* SHAO *following a retinue of*
GUARDS, *greeted by* DUAMMU *and* A-MENG.)

DUANMU & A-MENG: (*making obeisance*) My lady and my lord.

XIAHOU and SHAO: At ease.

(*They enter the mansion and take their seats.*)

XIAHOU: How now, my lord Duanmu, why is your son hurt?

DUANMU: O, my heart is cracked, cracked!

SHAO: So the news is true? A-Jia really sought your life?

DUANMU: Shame would have it hid.

XIAHOU: A-Meng, I hear you have shown your father a child-like
office.

A-MENG: It was my duty, sir.

DUANMU: He did betray this vicious practice, and was hurt while
trying to arrest him.

XIAHOU: All right. Send out arrest warrants immediately, set a
watch on every road. He must be decapitated in public to
make an example.

DUANMU: I thank your highness.

SHAO: (*looking askance at him with a smile*) You, A-Meng, are
exemplary. We appreciate your filial piety. A filial son

makes a loyal official. What would you say if we now
appoint you the captain of guards of the inner court?

XIAHOU: (*agreeing*) Very well.

A-MENG: I thank your ladyship and your lordship. I shall serve you
truly, even in the face of death.

DUANMU: I thank your grace.

SHAO: My Lord Duanmu, we are sorry to have to visit you at this
late hour, but there's urgent business wherein we need your
advice.

DUANMU: I serve you, and would like to know more about it.

SHAO: My sister has sent message that our queen mother has
departed. If she comes here, just tell her I don't feel well
and have gone to bed.

DUANMU: This, well . . . this doesn't sound right.

XIAHOU: You just follow the order. Say no more.

(*Enter a* GUARD.)

GUARD: Her majesty is here.

(SHAO *and* XIAHOU *gesture and exit, followed by their
retinue.*)

(*Enter* EMPRESS, SITU (*disguised as* GONGSUN KAI),
FOOL, *and* ATTENDANTS, *greeted by* DUANMU *and* A-
MENG.)

DUANMU: I would have gone out to greet you had I known of your
coming. I crave your forgiveness. This way, your majesty.

(*They all enter the mansion.*)

EMPRESS: My lord Duanmu, I went to my second daughter's only
to find that she and the duke had come here of a sudden.
The loving mother awaits her daughter's service. Where are
they?

DUANMU: The Princess has a headache . . .

EMPRESS: Headache? We are the one who has a terrible headache!
No, not yet, maybe she is not well. (*aside*) I'll be patient
and won't act rashly.

FOOL: Auntie, you shall soon see how tenderly loving your other
daughter is!

EMPRESS: What do you mean?

FOOL: A sour apple is a sour apple. Unless its genes are altered, it
can never taste sweet.

EMPRESS: You mean—?

FOOL: Do you know why we have the features on our face?

EMPRESS: I—don't know.

FOOL: Why, so that "The eyes can see and the ears can hear from all
directions." Even things without taste or smell can be
meticulously differentiated.

EMPRESS: I—did her wrong.

FOOL: Auntie, can you tell how an oyster makes its shell?

(EMPRESS *shakes her head slowly.*)

Me neither. But I know why a snail has a house on its back.

EMPRESS: Why?

FOOL: Why, to put its head in, not to give it away to its daughters and leave its horns without a case.

EMPRESS: You . . .

(*Enter* XIAHOU *and* SHAO.)

XIAHOU: Hail to your majesty.

SHAO: Health to your majesty.

EMPRESS: O, beloved Shao, your sister is naught. She really grieves me.

SHAO: Be patient, your majesty. You must have misunderstood her.

EMPRESS: Eh? How's that?

SHAO: My sister's filial piety is well known. Can you blame her for restraining your riotous attendants when she has cause?

EMPRESS: She is a hussy!—Eh, how did you know that?

SHAO: Never mind. O, your majesty, you are old. Even though your days on earth may not be many, it won't do to be incoherent like this. In my opinion, you'd better—

EMPRESS: Better what?

SHAO: Better return to our sister and say you have wronged her.

EMPRESS: Beg her forgiveness? (*kneels*) Thus? (SITU *quickly helps her up*) This is most becoming indeed!

SHAO: This, your majesty, is indeed unsightly! As the saying goes, "Be patient a while, and the storm ceases; take one step back, and find an enormous world." Why should you make your own life difficult?

EMPRESS: Humph! We shall never go back. She would cut half of my attendants. Such an ingrate is she that I curse her to be struck by thunder and sent to the eighteenth circle of hell . . .

XIAHOU: What kind of language is this?

EMPRESS: . . . be thrown atop a mountain of knives and down into a cauldron of boiling oil, her eyes gouged and her tongue pulled out, her belly cut and her intestines washed, and her body covered with scabies!

SHAO: O, heavens! How could you say such things? So will you curse me in your rash mood.

EMPRESS: No, dear Shao, you shall never have my curse. You're a tender, filial daughter. You will not begrudge me my pleasures, cut off my train, even shut me out. You won't forget who gave you half of the kingdom, will you?

FOOL: (*aside*) The geese are flying south: Winter Solstice is followed by Great Cold![1]

(*sings a ditty*)

> **Rich parents treasures are,**
> **So, feed and dress them well.**
> **Poor parents are just weeds:**
> **No need to give them ought.**

---

[1] Winter Solstice falls approximately on December 21, Great Cold on January 21.

We're doomed by star signs, we.

Why suffer in this world?

SHAO: Your majesty, let's face it—

(*Enter* SHANGGUAN, *brought in by a* GUARD.)

SHANGGUAN: Your highness, Princess Xu has arrived.

SHAO: Ah, indeed it's my sister. (*steps forward to greet her*)

(*Enter Princess* XU.)

EMPRESS: (*to* XU) Are you not ashamed to look upon us? (SHAO

and XU *take each other's hand, intimately.*) O, dear Shao,

will you take her by the hand?

XU: How have I offended, your majesty, to deserve this abuse?

EMPRESS: Unfilial hussy! You make me mad!

SHAO: I pray you, return and sojourn with my sister. O your

majesty—

(*sings*)

> **Since you are now so old, please act your age.**
>
> **To be headstrong does you no good at all.**
>
> **We will in turn look after all your needs—**
>
> **And there's no harm in cutting flunkies off.**

EMPRESS: No!—

(*sings*)

> **'Twas all agreed when I split up my land.**
>
> **How heartless is the thing that you propose!**
>
> **Though I must starve or die out in the cold,**

> **I'll never bow before this** (*points to* XU) **cruel wolf.**

XU: Eh?—

> (*sings*)

>> **It's only right one hundred lawless knights**
>> **Be disciplined, the house in order put.**
>> **To stay or not—you'd better think it through;**
>> **No need to harp on how you gave us land.**

EMPRESS: O heavens, how could I have begotten such a daughter?

> "My true love for your majesty, my mother" indeed!

> (*sings*)

>> **Cruel and ruthless demon**
>> **With a heart of stone and iron made!**
>> **You did profess obedience and love,**
>> **But normal human feelings now forget.**
>> **May you repent and learn mere courtesy,**
>> **So I have no regret for rearing you.**

> (*speaks*) I will not trouble you anymore. Farewell, we'll no more meet. I can stay with your sister, I and my hundred knights.

SHAO: Wait a minute, your majesty. You are mistaken. I am not yet provided for your fit welcome. Give ear, mother, to my sister.

EMPRESS: Is this sincerely spoken?

SHAO: I'll avouch it. And how about fifty followers? Why should you need more? That would only cause trouble.

XU: Your majesty, why don't you receive attendance from her
servants, or mine?

SHAO: Why not, your majesty? If then they chanced to slack you,
we could control them. If you come to me next month, I
entreat you to bring just five and twenty: to no more will I
give place.

EMPRESS: I gave you all—

XU: And in good time you gave it.

EMPRESS: With five and twenty? Say you so, Shao?

SHAO: Yes, your majesty: no more.

EMPRESS: (*to* XU) Then I'll return with you. Your fifty doubles
five and twenty, and you are twice her love.

XU: Your majesty, what need you five and twenty? Or ten, or five?
There's enough in the palace to tend you.

SHAO: She is right. What need one?

EMPRESS: Silence! You—you heartless, ruthless beasts! Reason
not the need!

(*sings*)

> **If simple roof can keep off wind and cold,**
> **What need have you of splendid walls so fine?**
> **If common weeds can keep your body warm,**
> **What need of silk embroidered for a show?**
> **Poor beggars sad who plead for food and home—**

E'en they have in their keep a few odd rags!

If one has just the barest things one needs,

How can one find one moment of delight?

(*speaks*) You heavens! Is this what you mean by "every thought of mine goes to you"? "I'd even catch the moon and the stars for you"—Ha! That's superfluous indeed! See how these two beasts treat their old queen mother!

(*madding*) Heaven and earth, if you are sensible, punish these traitors!

(*Thunders from afar, followed by stormy rain.*)

O you gods! You would make me die of heartbreak?

(EMPRESS *rushes off, closely followed by* DUANMU, SITU, FOOL, *and* ATTENDANTS.)

XIAHOU: (*looking out of the door*) It's going to be a big storm.

SHAO: This house is little; the old woman with her people cannot be well bestowed.

XU: She herself is to blame. Foolish and stubborn, she has put herself in these straits.

SHAO: Herself alone will I receive gladly, but not her followers.

XU: So am I purposed.

(*Re-enter* DUANMU.)

DUANMU: Her majesty is in a fury.

XIAHOU: What would she do?

DUANMU: Her majesty called to horse. I wonder where to?

XIAHOU: Leave her to herself.

XU: Yes, she may go where she wants to. My lord, by no means
    entreat her to stay.

DUANMU: Alack, the night comes on, the high winds ruffle, and for
    many miles about there's scarce a tree.

SHAO: Sir, to willful people the injuries they court will teach them
    lessons.

XIAHOU: Exactly. Better shut up your doors, my lord, to keep off
    the storm.

    (SHAO *and* XU *exchange glances, laughing knowingly,*
    and exit, followed by the others, except DUANMU *and* A-
    MENG, *who remain on stage.*)

DUANMU: This is unnatural dealing, A-Meng. How could they treat
    her majesty like this?

A-MENG: Most savage and unreasonable!

DUANMU: Go to, say you nothing. (*looks around, then in low voice*)
    I have just received a letter, which I have locked in my
    closet. Just wait and see: within three days Helian's power
    will be here. We should be loyal to the empress. I'll go look
    for her majesty and keep her safe. Go you to talk with the
    princesses and the duke, so that they don't perceive my
    plan.

A-MENG: Yes.

DUANMU: Be careful, A-Meng! (*exit in a hurry*)

A-MENG: Humph, a cringing old fool! (*sinisterly*) Ha ha!

(*sings*)

> **The heart of loyal courage shows a fool;**
> **He treats the warnings as a puff of wind.**
> **His trick I'll turn and use against himself,**
> **And so perform a deed of merit great.**

(*Light dims.*)

[Intermission]

Scene 5: The Storm

(Location: the wilderness.)

(*Circular projection showing a dark night of thunder, wind, and rain. Shivering chill descends on all sides.*)

[Chorus, *offstage*]:

> No sun, nor moon, nor even one poor star:
> Oh, certainly the world's now out of joint.
> When love and morals hold no longer sway,
> The state itself spins wild and turmoil reigns.

EMPRESS: (*sings, offstage*)

> Whipping and piercing is the rumbling wind;

(*Enter* EMPRESS, *followed by* FOOL.)

(*continues singing*)

> And spattering, the spouting, pelting rain.
> Deep fog: a night of cloud and sightless mist;
> Indistinct: sprays of water and of tears.

FOOL: In, auntie, and flatter your daughters. Better in a warm house than in such wind and rain.

EMPRESS: (*as if not hearing him, continues to sing*)

> Inconstant and degenerating world,
> I guarded not against your sycophants.

> **Alas, her mind confused, her bleeding heart,**
>
> **This white-haired woman's stricken with grief.**

[Voice-over]: (*getting louder and louder*) Unfilial daughter! Unfilial
daughter! Unfilial daughter! Unfilial daughter! Unfilial
daughter! Unfilial daughter! . . .

EMPRESS: (*continues singing; explodes*)

> **O wrathful skies, bring down your thunderbolts;**
>
> **Destroy now at once all the living things!**

FOOL: Auntie, he that has a little tiny wit would go back.

EMPRESS: No, never will I go back! Are these winds and rains
aimed at me? (*looks up at the sky*) Are you servile ministers
against me? Ha ha! No, no, I—I can stand it. Let fall your
horrible pleasure, you fools!

FOOL: He is a fool indeed that tries to prove his courage now. Winds
and rains pity neither good man nor bad.

EMPRESS: (*shouts at heaven*) Strike at the heartless beasts, if you
can!

(*sings*)

> **Let earth in fury crack and heaven quake,**
>
> **Split wide this evil world then make it new.**
>
> **Raise sudden storm to punish evil man,**
>
> **So perjurers can find no place to hide.**
>
> **Do not show off your potency to me:**
>
> **For cowards harm the good and fear the bad!**

(*Enter* SITU *disguised as* GONGSUN KAI.)

SITU: (*looking aroud; loudly*) Your majesty, your majesty . . .

FOOL: (*waving his hands*) Here, she's here!

SITU: Good heavens! Your servant has finally found you. Such
    dreadful weather, how torturous!

FOOL: Didn't I tell you?

SITU: Your majesty, hard by is a hovel that can shield you from the
    tempest. Rest you there, and I'll return to the princess and
    demand justice.

EMPRESS: I'm exhausted. My wits begin to turn. . . .

FOOL: "Keep the green mountain, and you'll always have logs for
    fire." Auntie, let's go to the hovel first.

EMPRESS: Yes, boy. (*to* SITU) Friend, lead us.

SITU: Come, your majesty.

    (*leads everybody to the hovel*)

    Get in quick, your majesty.

EMPRESS: Never mind me.

SITU: Please go in, your majesty. It's storming.

EMPRESS: This contentious storm, to me, is really nothing. The
    tempest raging in me is much more acute. My heart is
    broken to pieces! O Xu, O Shao, on such a night to shut me
    out? Your generous old mother gave you all—O, let me not
    think it, I can't bear it! Too debilitating! (*stumbles*)

SITU: (*quickly steps forward to steady her*) Please enter here, your majesty.

EMPRESS: Well. (*she takes a step, stops, and looks at* FOOL) My boy, are you cold?

(FOOL *nods, shivering.*)

I am cold myself. Poor boy! You go in first.

(FOOL *goes in, followed by* EMPRESS *assisted by* SITU.)

FOOL: (*groping around*) It's so dark you can't see your fingers. Here's some straw. (*starts making a bed with the straw*)

EMPRESS: (*feelingly*) Such weather! You homeless poor people—

(*sings*)

Your ragged clothes do scarce your body hide.

Hungry and cold, there's nowhere you can turn.

Now I myself in awful straits do stand,

How I regret my negligence of you!

May rich now shake their superflux to them,

And show the heavens more just.

FOOL: (*touching* A-JIA; *screams*) Ah, a ghost! (*hides behind* EMPRESS)

SITU: What's the matter?

FOOL: (*trembling*) A ghost—there!

SITU: (*steps forward*) What are you? Come forth!

(*Enter* A-JIA *disguised as a mad mendicant.*)

A-JIA: (*dancing wildly*) "Paraprajnama habodhisattva,[2]
    Mahakassapa Subhuti![3]

SITU: So it's a mendicant monk.

A-JIA: Go, as fast as ordered! "The demon, once it gives up the five
    desires, will be cleansed, and benefit countless beings."[4]

SITU: Full of sound and fury—what does it signify?

EMPRESS: Did you also give all to your daughters?

A-JIA: Just a pot of food, great teacher. Do some good, please. I've
    starved for two days, feeding on just one gecko. It's so cold.

EMPRESS: You didn't save anything? Gave them all? May heaven
    send down thunder to smash your daughters' heads!

SITU: The mendicant has no daughter, your majesty.

EMPRESS: Death, traitor! Who could have insulted, tortured him
    thus but his unfilial daughters.

---

[2] The Sanskrit for the Buddhist term is Prajnaparamita, meaning "wisdom" or
"omniscience" (prajna) and "crossing [over to the other bank]" (paramita). A-Jia,
no monk himself, makes a jumble of them.

[3] These are the names (in Pali) of two famous Buddhist monks.

[4] What the passage really means is this: "Once a bodhisattva has thoroughly
renounced the Five Desires (財，色，名，食，睡，lust for wealth, sex, fame,
food, sleep), all his defilements and obscurations will cease to be (will be
extinguished), and he will be able to bring benefits to countless sentient beings."
Again, however, A-Jia is not entirely clear about it.

For the elucidation of the original passage I owe a debt to Professor Tien-en Kao
高天恩, my long-time friend and colleague.

A-JIA: Beware of demons and fiends. I'm cold.

EMPRESS: Poor soul. Treat him well. These are mere borrowed
things. Off, off! (*tearing at his clothes while* A-JIA *rushes
toward the door*)

FOOL: Please, auntie, don't get mad. It's a naughty night to go—
streaking.

(*Enter* DUANMU *with a torch and a travel bag. He bumps
into* A-JIA.)

DUANMU: What are you?

A-JIA: Ah—(*recognizing his own father, he tries to hide, mumbling*)
in worn-out sandals, the great teacher swallows newts, dead
mice . . . (*hides in the corner of a wall*)

DUANMU: (*shaking his head*) A mad mendicant!

SITU: (*comes forward*) Her majesty is here.

DUANMU: (*to* EMPRESS) Here's my knee, your majesty.

EMPRESS: Are you—a sorcerer from the Land of Immortals?

DUANMU: Your majesty, I'm Duanmu, your old servant. Even
though heartless children treat their parents like weeds, I
have to keep my conscience and remain loyal and righteous.
(*takes off the travel bag and gives it to* SITU) Here are
some food and some clothes. Keep them. I have a carriage
ready. Please, your majesty, move to some safe place.

EMPRESS: (*holds on to* FOOL) Come, let's make a divination and
see our fortune . . . . (*they walk away*)

SITU: (*to* DUANMU) You see, my lord, her wits begin to unsettle.

DUANMU: Alas, can you blame her? Her daughters have abandoned
　　　　her. Lord Situ said it would be thus. He was right. In fact
　　　　I'm not much better. . . . I had a rebellious son, who sought
　　　　my life only lately. How grievous!

SITU: You take care, my lord. For now, let's help settle her majesty
　　　　first.

DUANMU: Yes. (*walks to* EMPRESS) Your majesty, your
　　　　majesty—please follow me.

　　　　(DUANMU *holds on to* EMPRESS, *who holds on to* FOOL;
　　　　they exit, followed by SITU.)

A-JIA: (*coming forward, pats his chest*) Good thing I wasn't
　　　　discovered. But—

　　　　(*sings*)

> **Something's amiss about her great downfall;**
> **And father's put a bounty out on my head.**
> **I live a life of naught save fear and dread,**

　　　　(*angrily hits one palm with his own hand*)

> **I hate the slanders of all villainy!**

　　　　(*speaks*) Alas!

　　　　(*continues singing*)

> **Prosperity' a dream; best give it up.**
> **I must go on pretending to be mad.**
> **When false is true, then true will false become.**

(*speaks*) I'll endure hunger and cold, beg for alms, till the day—

(*continues singing*)

I'll face the villain, and with vengeance, strike!

(*Light dims.*)

Scene 6: Gouging the Eyes

(Location: Duanmu's Mansion)

(XIAHOU *is reading a letter, with* XU *and* SHAO *by his side.* A-MENG *attends.*)

XIAHOU: (*reading the letter*) Humph, duplicitous traitor! Now I see it was not your brother's evil disposition that made him seek his death; he asked for it.

A-MENG: Your highness—

(*sings*)

> **How could I know he threatens from within,**
> **Conspires with foreign states us to invade?**
> **Ill fate to choose between family and state,**
> **Not be faithful son and subject good.**
> **The common's censure do I fear and dread,**
> **But over-tolerance breeds wickedness.**
> **That's why I must expose the secret plot,**
> **And make example of his wrong, I hope.**

XIAHOU: Such loyalty as yours is hard to come by. I'll thoroughly look into the case. (*hands the letter to* XU, *who reads it*) You're now promoted to general, with more rewards in store.

A-MENG: I thank your highness. (*hypocritically*) And yet—

(*continues to sing*)

> **Have pity on my dad's senility.**

> **Be lenient when his punishment you give.**

XIAHOU: Well. (*glances at* A-MENG) What a filial son!

Go, some of you, and bring the traitorous Duanmu before us.

(*Some* GUARDS *rush off.*)

XIAHOU: Sister, this business allows no delay. Please go back to your palace. Helian's army is invading, and Duanmu colludes with them. We need to get ready.

SHAO: Hang this old thief instantly.

XU: (*returning the letter to* XIAHOU) Gouge his eyes!

XIAHOU: Don't worry. I know what to do.

(*to* A-MENG) My lord, escort our sister home—this minute.

SHAO: (*glances at* A-MENG *and* XU, *is about to stop them*) That, er . . . that's perhaps improper . . . .

XU: Why improper? It saves General Duanmu the inconvenience of watching the interrogation.

SHAO: Well, then . . . then you must return as soon as possible—at this juncture, we need helping hands.

A-MENG: I do obey you.

XU: Get horses.

(*Exit one* GUARD.)

We'll go about business separately. (*Exeunt* XU *and* A-MENG.)

(*Enter* DUANMU, *brought in by the* 2ND GUARD.)

2ND GUARD: Your highness, the offender is here.

XIAHOU: Humph, put him on the rack!

(GUARDS *tie* DUANMU *on a rack.*)

DUANMU: What's this? What means your graces? What's the matter?

SHAO: Cunning traitor, playing innocent?

XIAHOU: Now, Duanmu, what have you to say?

DUANMU: Please, your highness, tell me plainly where I did wrong.

SHAO: Tsk, tsk, tsk. The duck may be dead, but its beak remains hard. Looks like he won't confess without some torture. Give him forty blows to begin with.

GUARDS: (*beat* DUANMU, *who cries out for pain and for injustice*) Ten! Twenty! Thirty! Forty!

DUANMU: Injustice!

XIAHOU: Injustice? Humph! (*shows him the letter*) This letter is hard evidence. How are you colluding with Helian? Speak!

DUANMU: The young princess is returning home to see her mother. How could you call this colluding?

XIAHOU: Quibbling!

SHAO: Nonsense!

XIAHOU: Where have you sent the empress?

(DUANMU *keeps silent.*)

SHAO: Speak, you old rogue!

DUANMU: Humph!—

> (*sings*)

>> **The savage storm a risky journey makes;**
>>
>> **Vast wilderness so harsh with biting cold.**
>>
>> **Because I could not bear to see her die,**
>>
>> **To borders dark I sent her in dark night.**
>>
>> **How could you blood relation so cut off?**
>>
>> **Of all good deeds, filial piety ranks first.**
>>
>> **Ignore it and by gods you will be damned:**
>>
>> **I'll wipe my eyes and wait to see that day.**

XIAHOU: Old fool, you'll never see that day—I'm going to gouge
out your eyes and stamp on them! (*takes out a knife*) Hold
him tight! (*The* GUARDS *do so.*)

DUANMU: Are you human? . . . (XIAHOU *takes out one eye;*
DUANMU *screams.*) Help! O you gods!

SHAO: One side will mock the other—that one too.

XIAHOU: (*laughing grimly*) "Damned by gods"? Now you know it!
(*about to gouge out the other eye*)

2ND GUARD: (*intervening*) Stop, my lord, hold your hand. This is
too cruel.

SHAO: How dare you, you dog!

XIAHOU: You fearless cur, eh?

> (XIAHOU *draws and goes at the* GUARD, *but misses. The*

GUARD *also draws, and hits* XIAHOU.)

SHAO: Seize him!

(GUARDS *swarm on* 2ND GUARD.)

2ND GUARD: (*to* DUANMU) My lord, you have one eye left to see his wound—a just retribution.

(SHAO *takes a sword and kills* 2ND GUARD.)

XIAHOU: (*despite the pain*) It won't be allowed to see anything. Out, vile jelly. (*gouges out the other eye*)

DUANMU: (*screams*) Heavens! Where are you, A-Meng? Do you see this? You must avenge your father!

SHAO: Out, treacherous villain! He is too good to pity you: it was he who, out of loyalty to the state, reported your treasons.

DUANMU: Ah—it was he? (*in dejection*) Then A-Jia was abused too . . . .

SHAO: Push him out of the gate and leave him to his own device.

(GUARDS *push* DUANMU *out.*)

(XIAHOU *stumbles, groans.*)

My lord, (*stepping forward to support him with her hand*) how is it?

XIAHOU: (*feebly*) I'm seriously wounded. Call . . . the doctor, quick!

(*Exit one* GUARD.)

SHAO: Careful, my lord. (*Exeunt all.*)

(*Light dims.*)

Scene 7: Evil Love

(Locations: Area A: Du Xu's Place; Area B: Duanmu's Mansion)

(Area A)

(XU *and* NANGGONG *in conversation.*)

(*Enter* 3ʳᵈ GUARD.)

3ʳᵈ GUARD: My lord, the army of Helian has advanced to our
　　　　border.

NANGONG: I see. (*waves his hand; exit* 3ʳᵈ GUARD) Well, we're
　　　　supposed to confront the approaching powers of Helian, but
　　　　they are led by our young sister, who claim she comes to
　　　　rescue her queen mother. What a dilemma!

XU: My lord, we need to make a decision quick.

NANGONG: Well . . .

　　　　(*Enter* SHANGGUAN.)

　　　　What news from our sister?

SHANGGUAN: Your highness, my lord Duke Xiahou is dead, slain
　　　　by his guard.

XU: (*shocked*) What?

NANGONG: A mutiny, was it?

SHANGGUAN: No. While gouging out the eye of Duanmu the

traitor, a guard, unable to dissuade him, drew his sword and felled him dead.

NANGONG: What? Gouged out his eye? That my lord Duanmu, so faithful, should meet with such fate—this is horrifying! Did he lose one eye?

SHANGGUAN: Both. The guard was killed on the spot, and Duanmu driven out.

NANGONG: The duke is dead—how true that "There are gods above us." Retribution comes speedily. But, O, poor Duanmu . . .

XU: My lord, in this urgency, we should get ready for the war! Why this useless talk?

NANGONG: How could you say so? Whatever we do, "reasonableness" comes first. My brother-in-law overdid his cruelty . . . .

XU: Well, my lord, go get ready for the battle. Jabbering and chattering can wait. . . .

NANGONG: Alas, the common people are the ones that suffer from wars. (*Exit.*)

XU: Such a wimp! Irresolute! No comparison with the handsome and smart A-Meng . . . (*smiles*) On the way back, how considerate he was! (*thought turning*) O no! Now that my sister is widowed, the deployment of the forces . . . (*in thought*) When a man and a woman, alone in one room,

with one heart against the enemy . . . they are likely to fall
in love with each other. What if A-Meng falls into her trap?
What then happens to my plan? No, I have to think of a
way to deal with this once and for all . . . . (*musing*) Ah, yes!
(*she picks up a brush and writes*)
(*sings an aside*)

> **A high-born lady her own choices makes.**
>
> **How could a crow with such a phoenix match?**
>
> **Our vows my lord will surely not forget;**
>
> **We make a perfect pair, unparalleled.**
>
> **A roc can fly above to clouds aloft,**
>
> **So you, my love, should aim to go so high.**
>
> **To catch our enemy, we must set traps,**
>
> **Then side by side we'll rule the land for aye.**

(*seals the letter, speaks*) Depart this instant, steward, (*gives
him the letter*) and present this secret missive to young
General Duanmu in person. Say it is my command that he
follow the instructions.

SHANGGUAN: Yes. (*about to leave*)

XU: Come back!

SHANGGUAN: (*halts*) Your highness?

XU: It is not good that this blind villain Duanmu should be loitering
at large, for people may spread rumors. Go and proclaim
his arrest and, once arrested, execution. There's bounty for

this.

SHANGGUAN: Yes. (*Exit.*)

XU: (*pleased with herself, smiles*) Sister, O sister, "If you don't guard
   your own interest, may heavens destroy you!" So, don't
   blame me for being ruthless!

(*Light dims in* Area A *and brightens in* Area B.)

(Area B)

(*Enter* SHAO *and* A-MENG.)

SHAO: (*charmingly*) You know, general—

   (*sings*)

   The duke unluckily has passed away,

   Which leaves the state both troubled and confused.

   The court requires an able minister,

   And I—I lack a dear and bosom friend.

A-MENG: Ya!—

   (*sings an aside*)

   Is this my lucky day to fall in love?

   Her speech, so strange—an overture to what?

SHAO: (*with provocative gestures, continues to sing*)

   Red candles and warm canopy of spring;

   In darkness, sleepless, moan I through each night.

A-MENG: (*continues to sing the aside*)

There's hidden meaning buried in her words.

Indeed the princess's love is very deep.

SHAO: (*offers* A-MENG *a cup of wine; continues singing*)

We'll drink fine wine, a pledge of our love:

Oh, love me tenderly as I love you.

A-MENG: (*takes the cup; continues to sing the aside*)

We'll share a single pillow e'en tonight—

As carp into a dragon roaring turns!

(*quaffs the drink, speaks*) With your favor, I'll perform my
best! Ha ha!

SHAO: (*in earnest*) My general, you must not disappoint me.

A-MENG: Rest you in peace, your highness. I will serve you—with
my whole self.

SHAO: (*as if suddenly reminded, in earnest*) Ah, A-Meng, there's
nothing between you and my sister, is there?

A-MENG: (*innocently*) What? Ah—of course not.

SHAO: Good. I can never endure it.

A-MENG: Fear me not.

SHAO: It's getting late. You . . .

A-MENG: Your servant will follow right after.

(*Exit* SHAO, *with an enchanting smile.*)

A-MENG: (*throws up his hands*) Both princesses love me. What
shall I do?

(*sings*)

To both did I my faithful promise give,
Yet only one of them at last I'll choose.
Both ladies are quite powerful I know;
My clever scheme can backfire easily.
The wind can change with ease, I know too well,
And wonder: Will it lead to weal or woe?
I'll stand aside as kin to kin they fight,
Escape like insect sloughing skin at night.

(*Light dims.*)

Scene 8: The Reunion

(Location: An open field)

(*Enter* DUANMU *with a stick.*)

DUANMU: (*groping along, fumbling*) O heavens—

> (*sings*)

> **The treacherous and double-dealing knave**
> **Has monstrous deed unto his father done.**
> **I stumbled as if blind when eyes I had,**
> **Suspecting not A-Meng's grim trickery.**
> **All dark before me now, though it's too late,**
> **My blindness gives a clarity—some joke!**
> **How I regret my biased, spoiling ways;**
> **The thought of honest A-Jia brings more grief.**
> **Oh now you heavens, open wide your eyes,**
> **And reunite good father and good son.**

(*Enter* A-JIA *disguised as a mad mendicant.*)

A-JIA: (*aside*) Ya! The man looks like Father. (*hides himself*) But
> why is he tottering?

DUANMU: (*grinding his teeth*) Cursed beast! Unnatural son!

A-JIA: (*aside*) Ya!—

> (*sings an aside*)

> **At this I tremble and shudder with fright;**
> **As father sings out curses angrily,**
> **And I can nothing do but silent weep.**
> **The villain slandered craftily.**

DUANMU: (*alert*) Someone there? Who's there? Don't hurt an old blind man!

A-JIA: (*aside*) What? Blind? I thought I was at the worst, but O world—the world is turned upside down! My father— (*continues to sing the aside*)

> **Why should he such a tribulation meet,**
> **To walk alone with such a searching stride?**

DUANMU: Who are you, anyway?

A-JIA: (*continues to sing the aside*)

> **I should go up and reunite with him,**

(*steps forward, then retreats; aside*) but no— (*continues to sing the aside*)

> **For safety's sake I'll keep in this disguise.**

(*speaks*) Hehe, the mad mendicant needs three bowls and one cassock.[5] Namo Mahāsattva, just freely give.

DUANMU: So it's the mad mendicant. We met in the stormy night. I thought . . .

---

[5] In fact, the mendicant monk needs one bowl and three suits. A cassock is a patchwork outer vestment worn by a Buddhist monk.

A-JIA: What did you think?

DUANMU: Alas, nothing. I was self-righteous in the past. I had eyes
that wouldn't see and ears that wouldn't listen. And see
what sad straits that has driven me to. So life is like a play;
nothing's constant in this world.

A-JIA: (*aside*) I don't understand. Look at him, his eyes are still
bleeding. I can't put on this false show anymore!

DUANMU: "Heaven is insentient; it treats all creatures as straw
dogs." How true!

A-JIA: (*aside*) And yet, I have to keep acting, however hard it may
be.

(*speaks*) Hey, reverend master, where are you going?

DUANMU: To the border. Know you the way? Can you lead me to it?

A-JIA: Ha! Of course! Horseways or footpaths, be they zigzag or
winding, I'm familiar with them all. But—hehe, a mad man
leads the blind, do you mind?

DUANMU: Not at all. That's just the way of the world. Since I've
nowhere to turn to, all places are the same to me.

A-JIA: Good, reverend master. (*gives his arm to* DUANMU) Follow
me.

DUANMU: Much obliged.

(*They walk about while doing some acts symbolizing
mountain-climbing or river-crossing.*)

[Chorus, *offstage*]:

> Father and son thus meet, unrecognized,
>
> Each holding back saddest tears of blood.

A-JIA: (*aside*) Look at him—

> (*sings an aside*)

>> Through empty eyes he moans and groans and
>> grieves,
>>
>> The mottled bloodstains wet, not even dried.
>>
>> The mountain's high, the river deep, and daylight
>> dim,
>>
>> We totter, teeter, as we trudge ahead.
>>
>> What happened, now my hardened heart must
>> know.
>>
>> With tact I'll make my father tell the truth.

> (*speaks*) Reverend master—

> (*sings*)

>> So rough, so very rough's the way.
>>
>> Why go you to the border far away?

DUANMU: Alas, you don't understand. This old man—

> (*continues to sing*)

>> A momentary slip, both eyes I lost.
>>
>> My loyalty's brought me to these straits.
>>
>> On traitors I'll see vengeful justice done
>>
>> By my petition to Helian Queen.
>>
>> This limping body struggles on in risk;

On tough roads I'll expose all treachery.

A-JIA: (*continues to sing*)

Whose false incrimination cost your eyes?

Whose scheme has put you into these awful straits?

DUANMU: (*continues to sing*)

My lying son, A-Meng. He set the trap,

And now good son, A-Jia, does suffer so.

An old and foolish man, I was abused,

And now injustice stains my son and me.

A-JIA: (*shocked, continues to sing the aside*)

Ah, damned villain, evil passed all words!

So, it's A-Meng—he's the hidden traitor, he!

So calculating, and so conscience free.

(*angrily*)

From this day forth he is no brother mine.

DUANMU: (*continues to sing*)

Too late I realized, I realized,

And now I am speechless and quite full of shame.

My face in vain I cover with old arms.

(*weeping violently*)

No end to tears when I think of A-Jia.

A-JIA: (*continues to sing the aside*)

In grief my father cries, to heaven sighs,

Revealing feelings true which break my heart.

Through my own tears I simply must call out—

(*speaks*) Ah, father!

(*continues to sing*)

Your loving son—now greets you on his knees!

DUANMU: Are you . . . are you A-Jia?

A-JIA: Yes, he!

DUANMU: A-Jia, O A-Jia! I did you wrong! (*feeling* A-JIA's *face; father and son embrace each other, weeping*) Is it really you?

A-JIA: Yes. I disguised myself as a mad mendicant, to keep from being recognized.

DUANMU: So the gods have eyes after all. Having seen you in my lifetime, I can die without regret.

A-JIA: Nonsense, father. Just relax. I believe the wrongs will be righted, and out of the depths of misfortune comes bliss.

(DUANMU *stumbles.* A-JIA *quickly steadies him.*)

Careful, father.

(*The two walks about a little more.*)

[Chorus, *offstage*]:

At last rejoined now are father and his son,

And hand in hand and heart to heart they walk.

(*Enter* SHANGGUAN.)

SHANGGUAN: By order of Princess Xu I've come to bring a letter to General Duanmu, but not a soul have I seen on the road.

Aiya! Wait a minute, up there—the eyeless traitor, a proclaimed prize! (*draws sword*) Ha ha, most happy providence! My eyelids have been twitching, a signal luck's been waiting; when Fortune comes your way, no one can say you nay! (*runs toward* DUANMU *in an attempt to kill him*)

A-JIA: Hold it! (*blocking him with the club he's been carrying*)

SHANGGUAN: Get out, stinking mendicant! Stay out of my good business.

A-JIA: Don't you bully the old man!

(*While they are fighting,* DUANMU *falls to the ground.*)

SHANGGUAN: Such skill? You're not a mendicant! (*looks closely*) You're Duanmu . . .

(A-JIA *snatches the sword from* SHANGGUAN *and stabs him.*)

SHANGGUAN: Ah!—then this letter . . . (*dies*)

A-JIA: (*helping* DUANMU *up*) It's all right now, father. Rest here a while. (*seats* DUANMU *on a rock*) Let me hide this rogue first, so none can find him. (*sees the letter as he drags away* SHANGGUAN*'s body*). Ah, this rogue is a messenger. (*opens the letter and read; shocked*) A letter to A-Meng? Well, it may prove most useful later. (*puts the letter away, then exit, dragging* SHANGGUAN*'s body*) (*Enter* EMPRESS, *disheveled and crowned with weeds.*)

EMPRESS: (*to a row of stones*) I am Empress of Xuanyuan—

(*sings*)

> **Soldiers of all ranks, now give attention:**
> **Your sovereign's here in greatness, to achieve.**
> **We gather now to loud drums thundering.**
> **Now follow us and—kill, kill, kill, kill, kill,**
> **Kill everything, and spare not even weed,**
> **Then celebrate when water's red with blood.**

DUANMU: That voice—isn't it—? (*shouts*) Your majesty!

EMPRESS: (*pays no attention to him but keeps looking at the stones*) Those people used to flatter me, replied "yea" to whatever I said. How obedient! But when the wind and the rain once disobeyed my command, chilling me, as the thunder keeps rolling, then I see through them. What the fawning dogs say doesn't count.

DUANMU: (*shouts again*) Your majesty!

EMPRESS: Come, you, come, come (*takes out a leaf and hands it to* DUANMU). Read for me this "Proclamations against the Rebels."

DUANMU: Your majesty, I cannot see.

EMPRESS: (*the leaf still in hand, impatiently*) Read it, quick!

DUANMU: Pardon me, I can't read with this case of eyes.

EMPRESS: Ah. (*turns around to size* DUANMU *up*) No eyes nor money, ha ha! How then can you be a matchmaker?

(*moaning*) Even Duanmu's bastard son is more filial than my daughters! (*harshly*) Better make matches at random. (*looking around*) Hush, see you the dogs are assuming authority?

DUANMU: I see it feelingly.

EMPRESS: That's it. If your eyes can't see, perceive with your ears. See you the bitch ascending the throne? A bitch is obeyed in office. That's called authority, you know.

DUANMU: (*wipes tears with his sleeve*) Your majesty!

EMPRESS: (*takes a look at* DUANMU) Well cried! I pardon you. When we are born, we cry that we are come to join the crowd of fools. On the snail's tentacles they all fight for fame and wealth. Do not cry. If you will, I'll give you my eyes.

DUANMU: O gods!

EMPRESS: (*despairingly*) Anyway, I have—(*in low voice*) no use for eyes . . . .

(*Re-enter* A-JIA.)

A-JIA: (*seeing* EMPRESS) Alas, her majesty is mad!

(*Enter* SITU, *undisguised.*)

SITU: (*shouts backward*) Dear Queen, her majesty is here!

WEI: (*sings offstage; then enters*)

> **Come back to Xuanyuan bitterly,**
> **To find her majesty I'm here detained.**

> **The sunsets are the same but people change.**
>
> **Her majesty looks so worn-out, unkempt.**

(*she runs to* EMPRESS; *kneels down; speaks*) O your majesty!—

(*continues singing*)

> **Never was one in such a sad shape!**
>
> **I swear my troops will fight until the end.**

EMPRESS: (*unbelievable*) Are you . . . the Supreme Goddess of heaven? Am I dead? (*She kneels, but* SITU *soon helps her up.*)

WEI: (*weeps*) Pardon me, Queen Mother, I've come too late.

(EMPRESS *prepares to go away;* WEI *stands up to stop her*) O you gods, cure her I pray! She is a mother driven to madness. Even my enemy's cur should have stood that stormy night by my fireside. How heartless you are, sisters!

EMPRESS: I've been dead; you shouldn't have waked me up. Where am I?

WEI: (*weeps loudly*) Mother, mother! Look upon me. (*she kneels*) This is Du Wei, your daughter Wei!

EMPRESS: Ah, pray do not mock me. I am a very foolish, fond old woman. I'm all confused. Do not cry. (*looks at* WEI *closely*) Are you indeed . . . my daughter Wei? (*she helps* WEI *up*)

WEI: (*wiping away tears*) So I am, I am.

EMPRESS: (*lowers her head as if in shame*) I have wronged you! I didn't give you anything!

WEI: Your majesty's well-being is the greatest gift.

EMPRESS: Am I in Helian?

WEI: No. In your own Xuanyuan. This punitive expedition of mine is sent, not to invade Xuanyuan, but merely to return justice to your majesty.

EMPRESS: Alas, I am old. As to justice—

(*sings*)

> **True justice—has this ever yet been known?**
>
> **My plans unwise have led to misery.**
>
> **Recall the day when I the empire split—**
>
> **You have full cause to hate me if you will.**
>
> **Regret and shame have struck me dumb and weak.**
>
> **A muddle-head, hopeless case am I.**

WEI: O your majesty—

(*sings*)

> **Still justice lives in human mind and heart,**
>
> **And piety no justifying needs.**
>
> **Your majesty must never speak such things,**
>
> **For I have long forgot divided land.**
>
> **A doctor we will find to make you well.**
>
> **We'll serve your majesty, and in deep bliss,**
>
> **Be happy and carefree for all our days.**

(*embraces* EMPRESS; *the two weep together*)

SITU: (*kneels*) Your majesty, here's the knee of your servant Situ.

> (EMPRESS *stares vacantly.*)

WEI: Please stand up, my lord. Her majesty's mind is not fully
> restored yet.

> (DUANMU *walks up, helped by* A-JIA.)

DUANMU: Your majesty, here's the knee of your old servant. (*about
> to kneel*)

WEI: (*supports him with her hand*) How you, in loyalty protecting
> your master, have suffered most inhumanly, I have learned
> from Lord Situ. Do accept my thanks. (*bows to* DUANMU)

DUANMU: (*returning the bow*) Not at all. I merely performed my
> duty. This is my son A-Jia here.

> (A-JIA *steps forward to bow to* WEI.)

WEI: At ease. Of the injustice done to your son, we are in full
> possession, and will make appropriate redress later.

DUANMU & A-JIA: Thank you, your majesty.

SITU: Your majesty, the troops of Xuanyuan are already massed.
> Please return to the camp and devise our strategy.

WEI: Well said. (*supports* EMPRESS) Mother, come.

(*Exeunt.*)

(*Light dims.*)

Scene 9: National Mourning

(Location: an open field)

(*The two armies are fighting. Dance formations. An assortment of sounds and lightings.*)

> [Chorus, *offstage*]:
>> **Brave banners cover sky and war drums roll,**
>> **While soldiers, chariots, crisscross the field.**
>> **Close fighting swells the scene of spirits brave;**
>> **Advancing warriors charge with cheery souls.**
>> **We hear outnumbered heroes' tragic shouts;**
>
> (*Enter* EMPRESS, WEI, FOOL, *and some Helian*
> SOLDIERS, *under guard.*)
>
> [Chorus continues, *offstage*]:
>> **As losers are defeated, winners crowned.**

WEI: Pardon, Queen Mother, your incompetent daughter!

EMPRESS: Never mind. (*waiving her hand*) From now on, just you
and me—

> (*sings*)
>> **In quiet and in peace we'll steal away,**
>> **From morn to eve close company we'll keep,**
>> **And watch butterflies through flowers wing,**

As two alone we'll intimately sing.

(*The two armies continue to fight, in silence. Helian*
gradually losing.)

WEI: (*touched, continues to sing*)

In voices low we'll whisper secrets sweet,
With truest heart I will dear mother please.

(*The two sides keep fighting, in silence; Xuanyuan*
resoundingly victorious.)

EMPRESS: (*pats* WEI *gently, continues to sing*)

The way of this sad world I clearly see;
When glory's shed, buds of truth appear.

A-MENG: Take them away.

(*Exit* GUARDS *with* EMPRESS, WEI, FOOL, *and some*
Helian SOLDIERS.)

Captain!

CAPTAIN: Here, my lord.

A-MENG: Send this order from Princess Xu: "As soon as the queen
of Helian is jailed, hang her. See to it."

CAPTAIN: Aye, my lord. (*exit*)

(*Enter* NANGONG, XU, SHAO, *and* GUARDS.)

NANGONG: General Duanmu, fortune as well your valiance has led
you in conquering the enemy. We shall duly reward your
merits. Now, where are the captives?

A-MENG: Sir, as your brother, I have ordered their arrest, awaiting further decision.

NANGONG: (*displeased*) "Brother"? I hold you as a subject, not a
brother.

SHAO: That depends on how we shall grace him. He led our powers,
bore the commission of my place and person, so he may of
course call himself your brother.

XU: Humph! Not so hot. By his own merit he does exalt himself, not
by your promotion.

SHAO: Humph! Certainly it is in our right to endow him. He can be
your peer.

NANGONG: Ha ha! Then he must first be your husband.

SHAO: (*coldly*) Jeers often prove prophets.

XU: Ha, silence!

SHAO: (*bending her abdomen*) Ah, the pain!

NANGONG: What's the matter?

XU: (*aside*) Humph, is it any wonder? That poison was specially
concocted by a shaman.

SHAO: I—

NANGONG: Sister, you don't look well. Do go back to the camp
and rest.

Come, someone, convey her to the camp.

(*Exit* SHAO, *supported by a* GUARD.)

(*Enter* 3ᴿᴰ GUARD.)

3ᴿᴰ GUARD: Your highness, a mendicant craves your audience.

NANGONG: A mendicant?—Bring him in.

> (*Enter* A-JIA *disguised as the mad mendicant, with* 3RD
> GUARD. *He approaches* NANGONG.)

A-JIA: (*in low voice*) Mistake not, your grace. I'm not a mendicant.
Please step aside, for I have a secret to tell you.

> (*Surprised,* NANGONG *gestures and the two take a couple
> of steps forward.*)

NANGONG: What are you?

A-JIA: This is Duanmu Jia. I need to conceal my identity for now, so
please your highness.

NANGONG: (*looks at* A-JIA *closely*) Indeed it's you! (*in low voice*)
What secret?

A-JIA: Read this letter and your highness will know.

> (*He hands over the letter, and* NANGONG *reads it.*)

XU: A-Meng, why haven't you taken action?

A-MENG: What do you mean? Please your highness be plain with
me.

XU: (*stares at* A-MENG) What? Haven't you received the letter?

> (XU *converses with* A-MENG *in a low voice while*
> NANGONG, *as he reads the letter, gets angrier and
> angrier.*)

NANGONG: (*to himself*) Brazen hussy! How dare she to conspire
with A-Meng against my life?

A-JIA: Your highness, my father passed away the other day. His dying command was for me to clean up the house. Please grant me the right to duel with this unnatural A-Meng and avenge my father.

NANGONG: Well—all right.

(NANGONG *and* A-JIA *return to their former places.*)

(*solemnly*) We have received secret information that Duanmu Meng is conspiring against the state.

XU: (*shocked*) What's this nonsense, my lord?

A-MENG: That's a lie. What proof do you have?

NANGONG: The solid evidence cannot be denied. Here (*shows the letter*) is the proof.

(XU *tries to snatch the letter, but is prevented by* NANGONG) Don't think you can destroy the evidence!

XU: Humph! I am the princess. Who can arraign me? (*Exit in a huff.*)

NANGONG: Come, someone, watch her closely.

(*Exit* 3RD GUARD.)

A-MENG: Your highness, I am totally ignorant of whatever the princess has plotted.

NANGONG: No need to argue. We should have executed you this instant, but heaven has a just arrangement.

Now, we order that Duanmu Meng duel with the informer (*pointing to* A-JIA). (*to* A-MENG) "Evil can never prevail over justice." Now, with your sword, justify yourself.

A-MENG: Ridiculous! Me, to duel with a mad mendicant?

A-JIA: No mad mendicant, I am the personification of justice.

NANGONG: (*raises his sword*) Now!

A-JIA: Take this!

> (A-JIA *and* A-MENG *fight;* A-MENG *falls after a few passes.*)

A-MENG: (*feebly*) You . . . your fencing skill . . . what are you?

A-JIA: The gods are just! (*reveals himself*) I am Duanmu Jia, your brother whom you wronged.

A-MENG: Ah, that it should be you!

> (*All react in astonishment.*)

> (*Re-enter* 3ʀᴅ GUARD, *rushing.*)

3ʀᴅ GUARD: Terrible, your highness! Both princesses are—dead!

NANGONG: (*shocked*) What?

3ʀᴅ GUARD: Princess Shao drank the poison with which she had poisoned Princess Xu.

A-MENG: (*with a bitter smile*) Ha, by gods' arrangement, we three are married in an instant.

NANGONG: How retribution has manifested itself!

> (*Enter* SITU, *fumbling.*)

SITU: Your highness, I am come to bid her majesty farewell before my long journey. Is she not here?

NANGONG: Great thing by us forgot! Come, someone, run to the prison and release her majesty and the queen of Helian. Escort them here.

A-MENG: "The dying man's words are good."—Run, for Princess
Xu did order the death of the queen of Helian.

NANGONG: Damnation! (*to the* GUARDS) Run! Hasten for your
life!

(*Exit a* GUARD.)

A-MENG: Alas, all my schemes have been in vain, and come to . . .

(*dies*)

A-JIA: Nothing.

NANGONG: (*gestures*) Take him away.

(*Exit a* GUARD, *dragging* A-MENG's *body.*)

My lords, this unfortunate land, completely devastated,
requires reconstruction. For us, we shall resign and to her
majesty grant our power. For the moment, however, it is
most important that you, with your great ability, help revive
this land. (*to* A-JIA) My lord Duanmu, please inherit your
father's title and place, and help us take care of the people.

A-JIA: Aye, I will do my best.

(*Enter two* GUARDS *carrying* WEI, *followed by*
EMPRESS *and* FOOL.)

EMPRESS: My dear, dear daughter! Why don't you say something?

FOOL: Auntie, restrain your grief. Once dead, man cannot come
back to life.

EMPRESS: O heavens!—

(*sings*)

My tears fall down and O the pains bite deep;

My calls my gentle daughter can't recall!

I seem to see her, kind and full of grace:

So straight she stood, like cypress or like pine.

But now she's cold as frost in withered death,

And leaving her mother in endless rue.

(*weeping, speaks*) My dear daughter—

(*continues the song*)

O heaven, when will we stop killing our kin?

How can the beanstalk bear to burn the bean?

O heaven, are not ethics life's cornerstone?

Foundations of our country turned to trash?

O heaven, where is justice in this world?

Is retribution mere fantastic talk?

O heaven, are there rules that govern life—

A momentary dream that none can trust?

Since human love is only paper-thin,

Behind your back by flatterers you're scorned.

With no reluctance this dull life I leave,

A carefree, unconstraining world to find.

(*speaks*) My daughter Wei, wait for your mother! (*stumbles and dies*)

(*Everyone is shocked.* 3ᴿᴰ GUARD *goes up to check.*)

3ᴿᴰ **GUARD:** Your highness, her majesty is—gone!

NANGONG: (*looking up to heaven*) Alas, unfortunate Xuanyuan! A
general woe!

(*He kneels, then everyone kneels.*)

(*Light dims.*)

(*Scene carries on into* Epilogue.)

Epilogue

(FOOL *walks downstage.*)

FOOL: (*seriously, sings*)

> One moment's slip destroys one whole state;
>
> How sad to be thus toyed with by gods!
>
> As sentient creatures mourn their own lost kind,
>
> To them I offer my libation, wine.

(*pours the wine*)

(*to the audience, continues singing*)

> In silence, fallen petals, rivers drift.
>
> How many histories destroyed be?
>
> If somehow you are moved by this sad play,
>
> Go spread the word about it through each day.

(*Light dims.*)

The end

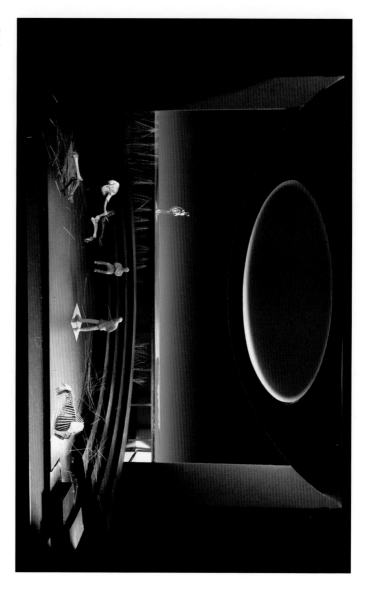

舞台二

天 問

（改編自莎士比亞《李爾王》）

彭鏡禧
陳　芳　著

臺灣學生書局印行

國家圖書館出版品預行編目資料

天 問

彭鏡禧‧陳芳著. – 初版. – 臺北市：臺灣學生，2015.11
面；公分
ISBN 978-957-15-1687-5 (平裝)

854.5   104021648

天 問

著 作 者：彭　鏡　禧　　‧　　陳　　芳
著作權所有：彭鏡禧、陳芳　cueariel@gmail.com
封 面 題 字：莊　　　千　　　　慧
出 版 者：臺 灣 學 生 書 局 有 限 公 司
發 行 人：楊　　　雲　　　　龍
發 行 所：臺 灣 學 生 書 局 有 限 公 司
　　　　　臺北市和平東路一段七十五巷十一號
　　　　　郵 政 劃 撥 帳 號 ： 0 0 0 2 4 6 6 8
　　　　　電　話：(0 2) 2 3 9 2 8 1 8 5
　　　　　傳　眞：(0 2) 2 3 9 2 8 1 0 5
　　　　　E-mail : student.book@msa.hinet.net
　　　　　http : //www.studentbook.com.tw
本 書 局 登
記 證 字 號：行政院新聞局局版北市業字第玖捌壹號
印 刷 所：長 欣 印 刷 企 業 社
　　　　　新北市中和區永和路三六三巷四二號
　　　　　電　話：(0 2) 2 2 2 6 8 8 5 3

定價：新臺幣三○○元

二 ○ 一 五 年 十 一 月 初 版

85404

ISBN 978-957-15-1687-5

《天問》由臺灣豫劇團首演
時間：2015 年 11 月 27-29 日
地點：臺灣臺北市國家戲劇院

導演	呂柏伸
技術導演	殷青群
邠赫拉	王海玲
都緒	蕭揚玲
都紹	張瑄庭
都維	謝文琪
端木格	朱海珊
端木加	張翊生
端木蒙	劉建華
司徒德	殷青群
優丹	鄭揚巍
南宮奧	連宏真
夏侯康	胡昌民
赫連王	林文瑋
鮮于侯	林原茂
上官逢	杜雋豪
侍衛若干人	張育茂、李志宏、楊原青
	林文瑋、林原茂、蕭揚珍
舞者若干人	張揚蘭、孫儀婷、陳彥如
	郭原亮、鄧海蓮

音樂設計	張廷營
配器	陳金池
服裝設計	李育昇
舞臺設計	李柏霖
燈光設計	許家盈
影像設計	王奕盛

序：「絕望之歌」

約瑟夫‧格雷夫斯*

北京大學

世界戲劇與電影研究所藝術總監

陳　芳／譯

　　加西亞‧羅卡（Garcia Lorca）戲劇《血婚》（*Blood Wedding*）以此言作結：「驚聲尖叫的闇黑根源」（西班牙文是 "*la oscura raiz del grito*"）。[1] 較諸抽象語言，這個意象更能暗示莎士比亞《李爾王》所要表達的。驚聲尖叫開始於文字與苦難的

---

* 格雷夫斯是知名劇作家、導演、演員；編、導、演作品曾在美國、英國、法國、義大利、俄羅斯、紐西蘭、臺灣、中東及中國大陸各處等地演出。

[1] 譯者案：羅卡（西班牙名：Federico del Sagrado Corazón de Jesús García Lorca, 1898-1936），是西班牙著名詩人、劇作家。引句全文是：「這刀子不足一握／但它乾淨俐落地刺入／那突然受驚的肌肉／然後停留在一聲尖叫的／黑暗根源的顫抖處。」見王秋桂譯：《羅卡戲劇選集‧血婚》（台北：驚聲文物，1970）。

終結。巴斯卡（Pascal）*2* 也曾有類似說法，大意約略是：「那些無盡空間的永恆沉默嚇壞我了。」巴斯卡是我們最偉大的悲劇思想家：理性概念讓他陷入理性恐懼；莎士比亞則引領我們向前更進一步。他的《李爾王》給了我們悲劇詩，其中當然並未忽略理性元素，而是融入了感性。莎士比亞把劇中的理性元素根植於劇中角色的覺知，似乎就像神創造我們每一個人時所為。理智可以認知悲慘情況的恆久神祕，可以畏懼它們，但只有軀體能經歷悲劇所有的感覺，能發現理性對無法解釋之物的恐懼轉換成令靈魂顫慄的敬畏，以及，隨之而來的，尖叫。

　　彭鏡禧與陳芳為自己設定了從莎士比亞《李爾王》英文轉譯成中文的巨大工程——這項工作本身就是極大的考驗。繼之在那重大考驗外，還要設法運用豫劇蘊含的在地文化知覺元素，以捕捉《李爾王》悲劇詩的整體於他們的改編作品——《天問》。

　　他們優異的作品在任何層面上都十分成功；毋庸置疑，今後多年，中文觀眾和讀者均可獲益於他們文學的、詩意的及戲劇的創作。他們保存了《李爾王》故事的完整格局，又維持改編作品可以處理的搬演長度，這分功力非常卓越。特別是在接近終場的戲劇行動，融合《李爾王》許多場景為少數場次，不僅精彩靈巧，且強力有效。這是兩位純熟勤勉的轉譯者的作品；他們就是真正的藝術家。

---

2 譯者案：巴斯卡（Blaise Pascal, 1623-1662），是法國知名數學家、物理學家、神學家及哲學家。

　　皮埃爾－艾米耶・杜夏（Pierre-Amie Touchard）3對於悲劇
這個現象有一巧妙的簡易說辭。他稱之為「絕望之歌」。我一直
認為那說辭是個精美的弔詭，因為悲劇並不歌唱。如果一個絕望
的人開始唱歌，他已在超越絕望。他的歌就是超越。但鏡禧與芳
讓我重新思考杜夏的措辭，緣於他們的《李爾王》改編是一首壯
麗的絕望之歌：如實歌唱是這部深刻動人的悲劇詩極為重要的組
成部分。

　　謹此向彭鏡禧與陳芳致謝：為了他們令人興奮的獨一無二、
優美奇異的改編／創作──《天問》。

3譯者案：杜夏（Pierre-Amie Touchard, 1903-1987）長期關注藝術教
　育。

〔弁言〕

於無聲處聽驚雷：
《天問》李爾王

落花無言隨流水
多少青史盡成灰
——《天問・尾聲》

「原創」與「改編」

　　莎士比亞（William Shakespeare, 1564-1616）創作於1603-1605年的《李爾王的悲劇》（*The Tragedy of King Lear*，以下簡稱《李爾王》）[1]，從表面看來，似乎就是一個頑固暴躁的老父親被不孝女活活氣死的故事；當然，因為這個老父親湊巧是個國王，這齣戲的意涵與格局也就擴大了許多。即便如是，此類討論孝道的內容，在中國傳統文化或戲曲中可謂汗牛充棟，不勝枚舉。那麼，改編《李爾王》還有什麼意義？

---

[1] 本文所據中譯本為彭鏡禧新譯《李爾王》（北京：外研社，2015）。

　　現今所知莎翁將近四十部劇作，大多是改編。例如《哈姆雷》（*Hamlet*）至少有四種主要來源；《威尼斯商人》（*The Merchant of Venice*）也和喬凡尼（Ser Giovanni）於 1588 年出版的義大利短篇小說有關；《量·度》（*Measure for Measure*）故事可上溯至辛席歐（Giraldi Cinthio）1565 年出版的《故事百則》（*Hecatommithi*）等。《李爾王》則明顯脫胎自 1605 年出版的《雷爾王紀年》（*The Chronicle History of King Leir*）；而在此之前，還有數種不同面目的傳奇流傳民間。難怪美國劇作家查爾斯·密（Charles Mee）在「（再）書寫計畫」（the (re)making project）中明示「沒有所謂原創劇本」（"There is no such thing as an original play"）：任何劇作都是其來有自的；即使是書寫自以為具有原創性的故事，也難以迴避文化銘刻的影響。可見「原著」與「改編」只是一種相對的概念。「改編」在媒介（medium）、樣式（genre）、架構（frame）、背景（context）等多方面均有大幅轉換（extensive transposition），必然異於「原著」。因此，誠如赫全（Linda Hutcheon）在《改編理論》（*A Theory of Adaptation*）中的呼籲：改編具有自我的獨立性，宜「視改編如改編」（Treating Adaptations as Adaptations），不能再用是否「忠於原著」的批評理論（fidelity criticism）去衡量。

　　莎翁的《李爾王》於 1606 年首演後，也許是緣於其中充滿了難解的人生課題，並未得到太多關注。大半個世紀過去後，愛爾蘭劇作家泰德（Nahum Tate, 1652-1715）還據此再改編為一個皆大歡喜的圓滿結局。不但與李爾呼應的副線主角格洛斯特

（Gloucester）之嫡子愛德加（Edgar）救了三公主蔻迪莉亞（Cordelia），兩人結為夫婦共治王國；且李爾和格洛斯特都能平靜地安享晚年。喜劇版《李爾王》在英國舞臺上大約風光了一百五十年，直到二十世紀，莎劇版的嚴肅性才真正被世人看見。

李爾三跪與救贖

現今舉世公認《李爾王》是莎翁最偉大的悲劇，也是戲劇演員終生難以超越的挑戰。畢竟能兼具王者氣度與生命厚度，在大喜大悲中演繹人生況味者，並不多見。《李爾王》凡五幕二十三場，寫於詹姆士一世（James I）兼攝蘇格蘭、英格蘭王位後，並曾在宮中獻演。故事背景設定雖是遠古基督教尚未創立以前，但隱喻大一統王國不宜分裂，否則後果不堪設想的寓意，卻相當明顯。莎翁此劇肯定詹姆士一世統治的重要性，是符合當時政治氛圍的（亦即政治正確）。當然也可能是如新歷史主義學派大師葛林布萊（Stephen Greenblatt）在《推理莎士比亞》（*Will in the World: how Shakespeare became Shakespeare*）中說的：莎翁及其同時代人退休時必須交出產業，轉而成為平凡年老的寄居者時，表現內心焦慮的一種方式。無論如何，《李爾王》對於人性表裡不一的刻畫、物質與精神的混淆、權力／利的掌控分配、真（自然）、假（虛偽）的觀察等，都有精闢的描述；而全劇的核心意義，顯然還是在於李爾的生命成長——因為掌權太久，剛愎自用，在以錯誤的方式交出政權後，墮入痛苦的深淵。經過委屈、憤怒、詛咒的階段，他逐漸學習接受、容忍人生的苦難，並從中

得到教訓，領悟同理心的重要，為自我找到救贖和新生的可能。暴風雨一景，正是李爾找回「人性」的轉捩點。

　　莎翁安排李爾在全劇中下跪三次：第一次發生在第二幕第二場，他的「故作姿態」只得到二公主麗根（Regan）的反諷：「別這樣了：這把戲很難看」（"no more: these are unsightly tricks." 2.2.332）；第二次在第三幕第四場，外在暴風雨原象徵李爾內在的風暴，但瘋狂的李爾反而在暴風雨中逐漸清醒。步入茅屋避雨前，他跪下來祈禱、懺悔：「赤條條的可憐人哪……憑著你們上無片瓦的腦袋、飢餓的肚皮、／……如何抵擋／這般天候？噢，我從來沒有／關心到這個！……」（"Poor naked wretches . . . How shall your houseless heads and unfed sides . . . defend you / From seasons such as these? O, I have ta'en / Too little care of this! . . ." 3.4.31-39）第三次在第四幕第六場，李爾與蔲迪莉亞相會時，後者說：「用您的手按在我的頭上祝福我：／您不可以下跪。」（"And hold your hand in benediction o'er me: / You must not kneel." 4.6.60-61）可見蔲迪莉亞先下跪請求李爾的祝福，未料老父王也跟著下跪了——他是真心表達深沉的內疚。同場結束時，李爾甚至明言：「您必須容忍我。現在請您，忘記、寬恕：／我是既老又蠢了。」（"You must bear with me. Pray you now, forget and forgive: / I am old and foolish." 4.6.88-89）相較於第一跪憤怒不智的「做戲」，這時老王已然謙卑認錯。他的靈魂被痛苦淨化，認同了人之所以為人的素質。從此，李爾不再是高高在上的驕傲君王。他深刻體悟到「人之異於禽獸者」的一點仁心，亦即悲憫之心。而這正是《李爾王》劇力萬鈞的底蘊所在，

也是人文主義值得彰顯的價值。

眞情與假意

　　一般在《李爾王》中被視為不孝者——李爾的長女、次女，及格洛斯特的私生子愛德蒙（Edmund），難道是天生的壞胚子嗎？平心而論，他們都在父親的偏執與父權社會的僵化體制中，長期承受不公不義的對待。李爾雖以耳聞諂媚之言作為分疆標準，然而這不過是「假戲真做」。他在第一幕第一場分配好長女、次女的國土後，對最疼愛的小女兒說：「現在，朕的寶貝……你有什麼可說，來取得／比你兩個姐姐更豐盛的第三份？說吧。」（"Now our joy . . . what can you say to draw / A third more opulent than your sisters? Speak." 1.1.74-78）既然早已畫好「比你兩個姐姐更豐盛的第三份」，老父王看似公平的分疆，實無公平可言。而愛德蒙限於身分被剝奪一切的怨懟，也在第一幕第二場一開始就展露無遺。他憤憤不平地說：「為什麼我必須／忍受可厭的習俗，容許吹毛求疵的／社會來剝奪我的權益，只因為／我比哥哥出生晚了十二三個月？／為什麼叫野種？為什麼是賤貨？……」（"Wherefore should I / Stand in the plague of custom and permit / The curiosity of nations to deprive me / For that I am some twelve or fourteen moonshines / Lag of a brother? Why bastard? Wherefore base? . . ." 1.2.2-6）這些「創傷記憶」，隨著年齡的增長而愈益積累，使得這對姐妹和私生子早已心性扭曲，人格發展不全。日後他們同聲連氣，貪婪冷酷，固然由於人為，但體制的規範也必有關連。

作為李爾鏡像人物的格洛斯特，後來轉向斯多葛（Stoic）學派「逆來順受」的人生觀，尋求合適的死亡時機。自殺不成後，他接受愛德加的勸說，決定「今後我要背負／痛苦，直到它自己喊／『夠了，夠了』才死。」（". . . henceforth I'll bear / Affliction till it do cry out itself / 'Enough, enough' and die." 4.5.88-90）可惜這種想法也不足為恃。經過種種磨難，最後愛德加下了結論：「說出感覺，而非於理當說之言」（"Speak what we feel, not what we ought to say." 5.3.345）強調自然情感遠比理性規範更為重要；天性親情，絕不適合稱斤論兩。如果世人能夠體認及此，應可避免許多悲劇。

跨文化：必也正名乎

從《李爾王》改編為「豫莎劇」《天問》，在文化、劇種、語言、情節、表演等各層面，都要進行調整。儒家論治國之道，子曰：「必也正名乎！」即由「攝禮歸仁義」的理念，引申出為政須以「正名」（劃定「權分」）為本。一切政治秩序制度，均應以決定權利義務為目的，才能「天下有道」。且首重德治教化，絕不能以不正當的手段達到目的。《天問》原為臺灣豫劇皇后王海玲量身打造，基於其本工行當是花旦、武旦、青衣，故而塑造「旦行女李爾」。本劇大抵維持莎翁原著的雙線結構，除主線邘赫拉（即李爾）母女外，也保留端木格（即格洛斯特）父子情節線。〈風暴〉、〈剜目〉二場，分別是主、副線主角行經人生幽谷的橋段，遭遇打擊後各自成長。邘赫拉體會到那些無家可歸的窮人「（唱）衣衫襤褸不蔽體，飢寒交迫無所依。老身淪落

一至此，愧悔昔日不自知。寄語顯貴施賑濟，公道昭然本於
茲。」於是開啟了設身處地、苦民所苦的人道關懷。

　　而端木格被私生子密告，慘受剜目酷刑。蹣跚獨行之際，巧
遇瘋頭陀（即苦湯姆，長子愛德加喬裝者），遂有「瘋子引著瞎
子走」的深意。不過，原著的格洛斯特是決心棄絕這個世界，擺
脫極大的痛苦，萬念俱灰要到多弗（Dover）跳崖尋死；他對愛
德加只有一句臨終遺言：「如果愛德加還活著，啊，請保佑
他！」（"If Edgar live, O, bless him!" 4.5.48）。端木格卻不然，
儘管雙眸血漬斑斑，還是勉力撐持，要求瘋頭陀帶他去邊關：
「（唱）一時不察失雙眼，忠心竟然受顛連。討伐叛逆秉公斷，
面陳王后在赫連。拚卻殘軀向前趨，辨奸何懼行路難！」此即關
乎正統王道繼承權的「正名」思想。倫理的分量，果然是中國傳
統文化中不能承受之「重」。所以，邠赫拉最後乃有椎心泣血的
「天問」：

　　　　（唱）問蒼天骨肉相殘何時已？

　　　　　　　煮豆怎忍燃豆萁？

　　　　　　　問蒼天五倫莫非風雅體？

　　　　　　　治國容廢萬世基？

　　　　　　　問蒼天人間公義何處見？

　　　　　　　善惡報應豈無稽？

　　　　　　　問蒼天因緣了斷生與死？

　　　　　　　黃粱一夢惟存疑！……（第九場〈國殤〉）

眼見青史零落成灰，落花終究無言。一切徒然，只能留待他年，
再說是非——

後記：衷心感謝 Joseph Graves 總監於百忙中為本書作序，導演
呂柏伸兄提供寶貴意見，育昇、柏霖慨允將創作手稿收入本書，
臺灣豫劇團提供海報主視覺與題字。

目　錄

天　問

改編自莎士比亞《李爾王》

彭鏡禧、陳芳

人物表

邠赫拉　　軒轅國女皇
都　緒　　邠赫拉之長女
都　紹　　邠赫拉之次女
都　維　　邠赫拉之么女
端木格　　軒轅國重臣
端木加　　端木格之嫡子，後喬裝為瘋頭陀
端木蒙　　端木格之私生子
司徒德　　軒轅國忠臣，後改扮為公孫凱
優　丹　　邠赫拉之弄臣
南宮奧　　都緒之夫君
夏侯康　　都紹之夫君
赫連王　　赫連國國君，都維之求婚者，後為其夫君
鮮于侯　　鮮于國侯爵，都維之求婚者
上官逢　　都緒之總管

侍衞甲　　邠赫拉之部下
侍衞乙　　夏侯康之部下
侍衞丙　　南宮奧之部下
侍衞長　　端木蒙之部下
侍衞若干人（以服飾區別，分屬邠赫拉、南宮氏、夏侯氏、端木
　　　　　氏、赫連國）
大臣若干人
軍士若干人（亦可以侍衞取代）

場　目

序　曲

（軒轅國宮殿）

（眾侍衛、眾大臣、司徒德、端木格、南宮奧與都緒、夏侯康與都紹、都維依序就位，隨後邠赫拉以雍容華貴、傲岸天下之姿緩步上。筵席前開始歌舞表演）

【幕後伴唱】：百花爭豔送春暖，

　　　　　　九天閶闔鑼鼓喧。

　　　　　　冠冕奉觴太和殿，

　　　　　　萬壽無疆賀軒轅。

【接幕後獨唱】：至尊女皇世罕見，

　　　　　　　一朝分疆詔令頒。

【接幕後伴唱】：不知陛下怎盤算？

　　　　　　　滿朝文武屏息觀。

（下接第一場）

第一場　市愛

衆　人：（行禮）恭祝陛下聖誕千秋，萬歲萬萬歲！

邠赫拉：哈哈！平身。

（唱）自登基理國政獨斷乾坤，

轉眼間已然是一十八春。

苦征戰年復年心竭力盡，

御三軍不懈怠事必躬親。

好容易大一統萬民歸順，

享尊榮樂歡暢正待舒心。

祭天地告列祖誰堪大任？

朕決意軒轅國疆域三分。

（衆人紛紛點頭）

端木格：陛下日前已詔告天下，臣等盡知，有賴聖裁。

邠赫拉：如此甚好。

（向端木格）端木大人，朝儀已畢，去請赫連王、鮮于侯前來赴宴。

端木格：是。（下）

邠赫拉：取地圖來。

（一侍衞奉上地圖）

邠赫拉：衆卿家皆知，早年先皇體弱多病，朕不得不代為決行國事。爾後先皇駕崩，膝下並無子嗣，惟有三名幼女。彼時內憂外患，為了國家安定，朕只好暫登大寶。幸賴衆

卿輔佐，朕與爾等出生入死、南征北討，乃有今日四海
昇平。趁此盛會，朕有要事宣布——

（唱）續皇族血脈連至關根本，

　　　　創新猷異前代國祚長存。

（略停，綜觀全場）

　　　　三嬌兒各自道良善孝順，

　　　　賜恩惠、憑言語——朕絕不偏心。

眾　人：（大驚，面面相覷，竊竊私語）什麼？什麼？憑言語？
說好聽話？就能得到國土？

（邠赫拉使個眼色，侍衛甲上前）

侍衛甲：（大聲）肅靜！（退回原位）

（眾人安靜，望向邠赫拉）

邠赫拉：都聽清楚了吧？朕有意安享晚年，把政務交給三位公
主。誰更孝順，就可以得到更多恩賜。南宮奧、夏侯康，
爾等身為駙馬，也要襄助治國啊。

南宮奧、夏侯康：（對望一眼）遵命。

邠赫拉：緒兒，你是長公主，你先說吧。讓朕知道你的孝心。

都　緒：（上前堆笑）聖明的陛下啊——

（邊想邊唱）蓊鬱大樹好遮蔭，

　　　　　　慈母嚴父集一身。

（略停）軒轅異寶俱劣品，

　　　　皇娘原是稀世珍。

　　　　千言萬語訴不盡，

　　　　孝順皇娘情意真。

　　　　　　（眼睛咕碌一轉）早晚請安冷暖問，

邠赫拉：（滿意）好、好、好。

都　緒：（續唱）隨侍左右不離分。

都　紹：（旁白）哎唷，這般討好皇娘啊——我可不會輸給你！

都　維：（旁白）我該說什麼呢？但求問心無愧，何須夸夸其談？

邠赫拉：（指地圖）從西北到東北，這一大片富饒的山川、廣闊
　　　　的平野，朕都傳給你和南宮奧了。

都緒、南宮奧：謝陛下隆恩。

邠赫拉：現在輪到你了，紹兒。你怎麼說？

都　紹：（看都緒一眼，媚笑）親愛的陛下啊——

　　　　（唱）大姐與我同胞生，

　　　　　　　句句形容我心聲。

　　　　　　　我愛皇娘勝於命，

　　　　　　　念念牽引骨肉情。

　　　　　　　日日遊賞三春景，

　　　　　　　夜夜笙歌安樂宮。

　　　　　　　孝親還借東風送，

　　　　　　　上天直取明月星。

都　維：（旁白）啊，天可憐見！我這片孝心，惟神明共鑒。

邠赫拉：哈哈！你和夏侯氏子子孫孫，永遠繼承這壯麗江山的三
　　　　分之一。（指地圖）西南這一片的價值，可不亞於賜給
　　　　你大姐的。

都紹、夏侯康：多謝陛下洪恩浩蕩。

邠赫拉：現在，（向都維，語氣更溫柔）朕的愛女，你雖是遺腹

子，無緣得見父皇，朕亦疏於看顧，但朕留著最豐厚的
一分給你。不論赫連王或鮮于侯成為駙馬，都可以與你
共享這分嫁妝。來來來，說吧。朕等著呢。

都　維：我……無話可說。

　　　　（眾人訝異）

邙赫拉：（錯愕）無話可說？

都　維：無話可說。

邙赫拉：無話可說就無物可得喔。重說。

都　維：女兒何其不幸，無法誇飾言語，只能順乎良知來孝敬陛
下啊。

邙赫拉：怎麼回事，維兒？修正你的說辭，以免損失朕為你準備
的財富。

都　維：陛下，皇娘啊——

　　　　（唱）椿萱恩慈重，

　　　　　　　天倫古今同。

　　　　　　　回饋反躬省，

　　　　　　　量力惟盡心。

　　　　　　　豈能獨邀寵，

　　　　　　　巧言惑視聽？

邙赫拉：這可是你的真心話？

都　維：是的。（續唱）伏乞陛下鑒，

　　　　　　　　　　自然見真情。

邙赫拉：如此年輕卻如此寡情？

都　維：如此年輕，陛下，如此真誠。

邠赫拉：（怒氣沖沖）哼！你——你——

（旁唱）聞此言不由得七竅生煙，

不孝女據理爭忤逆當前。

信口開全不顧朕的顏面，

朝會中哪裡有皇室尊嚴？

（白）既然如此，你的真誠就是你的嫁妝。

（續唱）即日起母女情義絕恩斷，

發重誓朕昭告后土與皇天。

（全場驚訝，靜默片刻）

司徒德：陛下——

邠赫拉：住口，司徒德！

（續唱）可笑朕費周章一廂情願，

竟指望不孝女照拂餘年。

（白，向都維）滾，滾出去！朕沒有你這種女兒！

（都維退後數步）

（向侍衛）去叫鮮于侯。沒聽見麼？去叫赫連王。

（二侍衛下）

（向南宮奧、夏侯康）二位駙馬，除了公主既得的妝奩外，（指地圖）剩下的這一大片土地，也由你們平分了。以後，軒轅國就交給你們兩家共治。

南宮奧、夏侯康：是。

邠赫拉：但朕要保留國君的名號和排場，還有侍衛百名，按月輪住你們的宮殿。

（取出玉璽）來，這是玉璽，現在就賜予你們作為憑證。

（南宮奧、夏侯康上前接過玉璽）

司徒德：陛下，微臣一向服膺您的旨意，不敢違逆……

邲赫拉：朕心意已決，不必多言。

司徒德：陛下，請恕微臣無禮。即使浮雲蔽日，小人當權，微臣
　　　　也要直諫。請您收回成命吧。微臣敢以性命擔保，小公
　　　　主絕非無情之人。不善言辭，並非表示不孝。

邲赫拉：司徒德！不想活啦？住口。

司徒德：微臣向來效忠陛下。為您犧牲，在所不惜。

邲赫拉：滾出去！

司徒德：陛下，您會後悔的。

邲赫拉：噢，你這混帳！來人，拖出去斬了。

（眾人大驚失色）

南宮奧、都維：陛下，請息怒。

司徒德：陛下，請您三思。

邲赫拉：（氣極敗壞）哼，哼！你自認是忠臣，膽敢指責朕的不
　　　　是。好，現在就去收拾家當，滾出軒轅國。三日之後，
　　　　只要你還在國內，就格殺勿論。滾！

司徒德：也罷，君既不君，臣豈能臣？流放或許更好。願陛下福
　　　　壽安康，微臣告退。

　　　　（向都維）公主，保重。

都　維：（不捨）大人！

司徒德：（向都緒、都紹）願二位公主言行一致。

　　　　（都緒、都紹冷眼以對）

司徒德：（環顧四周）各位，告辭了。（下）

（一侍衛上）

侍　衛：啟稟陛下，赫連王、鮮于侯到。

（赫連王、鮮于侯、端木格上）

赫連王、鮮于侯、端木格：（同向邠赫拉行禮）參見陛下。

邠赫拉：平身。

（端木格歸位）

二位同時前來向小女求親，朕原是準備了豐厚的嫁妝。然而，現在她身價暴跌了。唔，（以眼神示意）她在那裡。

（向鮮于侯）鮮于侯，朕先問你：你還要娶她麼？

鮮于侯：（不解）陛下，臣只要求您曾允諾的部分。您也不會少給吧？

邠赫拉：她不再是朕的愛女了。不僅一文不名，還加上朕的嫌惡。如果你願意，就帶她走吧。

鮮于侯：啊？這……（望都維一眼）這真讓臣難以回答。

邠赫拉：這個無心無肺的小賤人，剛成為朕的仇敵。朕的咒詛就是她的嫁妝。你是要她還是不要？

鮮于侯：果然如此，那麼……（低頭）臣不敢高攀。

都　維：（旁白）眼中只有財富和權位，本宮也不願下嫁。

邠赫拉：（向赫連王）賢侄，先皇與令尊有八拜之誼，朕不便把憎惡之人許配於你。賢侄還是另娶名門吧。

赫連王：實實令人難以置信。陛下一直誇讚小公主是您最鍾愛的女兒，您的掌上明珠，怎麼霎時之間就犯了滔天大罪？她做了什麼傷天害理之事麼？

都　維：（上前兩步）求求您，陛下，請您明示。畢竟女兒只是
　　　　不善於逢迎諂媚，而非做了什麼寡廉鮮恥、傷風敗俗之
　　　　事，以致失去您的愛寵。

邠赫拉：哼，還要狡辯！連一句美言都吝於出口！朕寧願沒有生
　　　　你，賤人！

赫連王：只是這樣麼？不就是天性嫻靜，不善於花言巧語麼？看
　　　　看這位美麗的公主——

　　　　（唱）清新本天然，

　　　　　　　素淨如白蓮。

　　　　　　　紅顏多靦覥，

　　　　　　　楚楚惹人憐。

　　　　　　　眼底透幽怨，

　　　　　　　意態扣心弦。

　　　　（上前牽起都維之手，續唱）願效雙飛燕，

　　　　　　　　　　　　　　　結褵入赫連。

　　　　（轉向邠赫拉）陛下，人棄而我取，小侄願娶公主。

邠赫拉：哦？朕說過了，她沒有嫁妝。她一無所有。

赫連王：「窈窕淑女，君子好逑」——她本人就是最好的嫁妝。
　　　　既然公主不能見容於此，正好做小王的王后，共治赫連
　　　　國。

邠赫拉：好，你娶你的吧。朕沒有這個女兒，以後也不必再見。
　　　　儘管上路吧。

赫連王：（向都維）去道別吧，公主。

　　　　（都維上前欲拜別邠赫拉，但邠拂袖下，眾人隨下。端

　　木格似有話要説，終究未説，隨下。都緒、都紹留在原
　　地）

　　（趨前安慰都維）雖然他們無情無義，「失之東隅，收
　　之桑榆」，不必傷感。

都　維：（向都緒、都紹）二位姐姐，請好好照顧皇娘。

都　緒：這是我們的事。

都　紹：你還是操心自己吧。

都　維：我……

　　（赫連王搖搖頭，拉著都維下）

都　緒：（旁白）呀，這——

　　（旁唱）大喜過望乾坤轉，

　　　　　　無端到手半江山。

都　紹：（續旁唱）小妹失寵異域遣，

　　　　　　　皇娘行事忒倒顛。

都　緒：二妹，看來陛下今晚就會起駕。

都　紹：那可不？先去貴府，下月再到敝處。

都　緒：你看她是多麼任性！（上前牽起都紹的手，輕拍著）難
　　保將來不這麼對待你我。

都　紹：正是，遲早會害了咱們。

都　緒：咱們得想個法子。

都　紹：此事拖不得。

都　緒：（續旁唱）喜怒無常留後患，

都　紹：（續旁唱）天威難測臨深淵。

都　緒：（續旁唱）未知前途風波險，

　　　　　　是福是禍——

都　紹：（續旁唱）半憂半喜——

都緒、都紹：（合）心怎安？

　　（切光）

第二場　離間

（端木府邸）

端木蒙：（讀信上，得意貌，吟）「老賊專橫勝以往，
　　　　　　　　　　　　　　　現世尊老忒荒唐。
　　　　　　　　　　　　　　　吾輩徒然多忍讓，
　　　　　　　　　　　　　　　苦等不得百寶箱。
　　　　　　　　　　　　　　　平分家產非妄想，
　　　　　　　　　　　　　　　但送老爹見閻王。
　　　　　　　　　　　　　　　經年蹉跎終迷惘，
　　　　　　　　　　　　　　　不如及時共密商。」

　　　　　（唱）名利並非天生有，
　　　　　　　　　只合巧手暗裡偷。
　　　　　　　　　貴賤不必分長幼，
　　　　　　　　　庶子奪權自籌謀。

　　　　　（端木格從另一方向上）
　　　　　（看到端木格）哈，老頭兒來了。

端木格：（自言自語）司徒大人被流放？赫連王匆匆歸國？陛下
　　　　昨晚已離宮？放棄大權而寄人籬下？這一切何其突然！
　　　　（看到端木蒙）阿蒙，怎麼了？有什麼事？

端木蒙：哦，爹爹，無有，無有什麼事啊。（急忙藏信狀）

端木格：幹嘛慌慌張張的？

端木蒙：沒、沒有啊，爹爹。

端木格：你剛才看的是什麼信？

端木蒙：沒什麼，爹爹。

端木格：沒什麼？既然沒什麼，就不要遮遮掩掩。給為父看看。

端木蒙：求求您，爹爹，原諒孩兒。這封信是大哥寫的。小子以
　　　　為，您最好不要過目。

端木格：拿出來。

端木蒙：對不住您啊，這封信看不得。

端木格：拿出來！阿蒙，為父要看。

　　　　（端木蒙取出信來，端木格一把搶過）

端木蒙：但願大哥寫這封信，只是為了試探於我。

端木格：（讀信，詫異）「老賊專橫勝以往，現世尊老忒荒唐……」
　　　　咦？這是從何說起——

　　　　（唱）自從盤古開天地，

　　　　　　　尊老敬賢立綱常。

　　　　　　　小子何事亂吵嚷？

　　　　　　　直呼老賊忒荒唐。

　　　　（白）這信是何時收到的？哪個送來的？

端木蒙：無人送來，爹爹。孩兒一早在臥房地上撿到的。

端木格：你認得這個筆跡麼？是你兄長的麼？

端木蒙：假若內容恭順，爹爹，我敢發誓是他寫的。但寫成那樣，
　　　　孩兒——不敢說。

端木格：（端詳）是阿加的筆跡。

　　　　（續讀，續唱）算計家產當面搶，

竟要老夫見閻王？

（白）端木加？他寫得出這種信？他想得出這種念頭？哼，可惡！混蛋，混蛋！可惡的混蛋！傷天害理的禽獸！不，禽獸不如！

端木蒙：爹爹，興許他只是鬧著玩兒的，不是真心話。

端木格：（續讀，續唱）貪婪無厭使伎倆，

天地不容喪心狂。

（白）去，阿蒙，去找他。老夫要把他吊起來。這個沒天良的混蛋在哪裡？

端木蒙：孩兒不知，請您暫且息怒，先釐清真相再說。或許大哥只是要試探我對您的孝心。

端木格：你這麼想？

端木蒙：爹爹，不如孩兒略作安排，讓您親耳聽聽大哥怎麼說。

端木格：（搖頭）他不會這麼不孝。阿蒙，去找他，見機行事。為父一定要查個水落石出。

端木蒙：是，爹爹。

端木格：唉，這天象——

（唱）日月異常驚山鳥，

春來無故草木凋。

吉凶禍福知多少，

天人感應劫難逃。

父不父、子不子，

顧後瞻前、不由老夫不心焦。

（白）阿蒙，去找這個混蛋。小心行事。

端木蒙：孩兒這就去。爹爹請先回房安歇，等候消息。

端木格：嗯！（下）

端木蒙：蠢老頭！愚蠢之至。世人遭遇不幸，明明是自作自受，
　　　　卻要歸咎於天象。什麼天人感應？唔！真是推卸責任。
　　　　（端木加上）
　　　　他來得正好。

端木加：怎麼啦？蒙弟，這麼嚴肅，你在想什麼呀？

端木蒙：大哥，小弟正在研究卜卦，關於日蝕、月蝕之類的事。

端木加：（不以為然）你把工夫花在那玩意兒上？

端木蒙：是啊，這些卦辭都很精準哪。
　　　　你最近是何時見過爹爹的？

端木加：昨晚。

端木蒙：有談話麼？

端木加：有啊，約莫談了半個時辰。

端木蒙：你們道別時光景如何？他沒有動怒麼？

端木加：沒有啊。

端木蒙：你再仔細想想，哪裡得罪了爹爹？此時他正大動肝火，
　　　　就算宰了你也難消怒氣。小弟勸你先避避風頭吧。

端木加：嘎，有這等事？肯定是有哪個小人陷害愚兄。

端木蒙：我估計也是這樣。暫且委屈大哥，躲到小弟臥房。等他
　　　　氣消了，我再陪你去見父親大人。快走吧。
　　　　（端木加猶豫）
　　　　走啊。
　　　　（端木加匆匆下）

端木蒙：哼！宮中這些無知的傢伙，憑什麼說我是雜種、是賤貨？
我相貌堂堂，一表人才，長得也挺像父親，為何要烙上
雜種之名？私生子又怎麼樣？哼——

（唱）天花亂墜一張口，

　　　巧妙布置自成仇。

　　　只怪兄長太忠厚，

　　　父親也是蠢老頭啊、蠢老頭。

（白）哼！端木加，等著瞧！老子一定要揚眉吐氣，取
代你這個「合法的」蠢貨！哼哼哼！（冷笑不已）

（切光）

第三場　辱親

（都緒宮殿外）

（狂歡音樂起，眾侍衛分組角觝百戲；或吞刀吐火，或變臉跌撲，或扛鼎尋橦，或跳舞鬥劍。邲赫拉與數名侍衛喧譁嬉鬧上，掄槌擊鼓）

【幕後伴唱】：喧譁無度魚龍衍，

　　　　　　吉曜稱慶太平年。

　　　　　　驍勇健騎厭征戰，

　　　　　　終日揮霍賽神仙。

邲赫拉：（續唱）快意不覺天向晚，

　　　　　　嬉戲忘卻兩鬢斑。

　　　　　　風光正好償夙願，

　　　　　　退位無憂樂陶然。

眾侍衛：（大聲嚷嚷）餓了、餓了！一刻也不能等了！

邲赫拉：朕也餓了，快叫宮裡準備。

　　　　（一侍衛承應，下）

　　　　（司徒德改扮為公孫凱上）

司徒德：（整冠、理鬢，身段亮相）現在，流放的司徒德，已經易容為公孫凱。只要再改變口音，就可以在軒轅國繼續盡忠了。

（司徒德擋在邙赫拉之前）

邙赫拉：咦，你是何人？

司徒德：稟陛下，小人是個老實的好漢。

邙赫拉：你是幹什麼的？

司徒德：小人什麼都能幹。

邙赫拉：你想要什麼？

司徒德：小人想侍候您，為您效勞。因為您有一種威嚴，令人敬
　　　　服。小人情願為您跑腿、打雜、傳口信，求您賞口飯吃。

邙赫拉：哈哈，好個會說話的傢伙。這麼著，咱們先去吃飯，吃
　　　　飽了再說。

　　　　（率眾入宮，大聲）開飯吧！優丹呢？朕的弄臣在哪兒
　　　　呢？去叫他過來。

　　　　（另一侍衛承應，下）

　　　　（上官逢上，過場）

　　　　喂，喂，小子，緒兒在哪裡？

上官逢：（頭也不回繼續走）嗯嗯嗯——

邙赫拉：那蠢才嘟噥些什麼？叫他回來。

　　　　（侍衛甲承應下）

　　　　咦，朕的弄臣怎麼還沒來？人都到哪兒去啦？

　　　　（侍衛甲上）

　　　　怎麼，那兔崽子呢？

侍衛甲：陛下，他說他沒工夫。

邙赫拉：他沒工夫？

侍衛甲：陛下，不知何故，這些僕人似乎不如以往殷勤。就連公

　　　　主和駙馬，也都冷淡多了。

邙赫拉：嘎，有這種事？

侍衛甲：陛下恕罪，屬下職責所在，不能知情不報。

邙赫拉：你這麼一說，朕倒想起他們近來是有些怠慢。原先朕還
　　　　以為是自己多心呢。以後，你要幫朕多留點兒神。可優
　　　　丹呢？朕有兩天沒見到他了。

侍衛甲：陛下，自從小公主去了赫連國，優丹也憔悴了許多。

邙赫拉：不准再提此事，朕很清楚。

　　　　你去告訴公主，朕有話對她說。

　　　　（侍衛甲承應，下）

　　　　你去，叫優丹過來。

　　　　（另一侍衛承應，下）

　　　　（上官逢上）

邙赫拉：嘿，這位大爺，您，您請過來。

　　　　（上官逢擠眉弄眼，故意不理。司徒德上前拖他過來）

　　　　請問，朕是何人？

上官逢：（冷漠）我家公主的老皇娘。

邙赫拉：「我家公主的老皇娘」？你這奴才，你這狗雜碎！

上官逢：我可不是狗雜碎。

邙赫拉：你敢吹鬍子瞪眼兒，你這無賴？（打他一耳光）

上官逢：不可動手。

司徒德：也不可動腳吧，（絆倒他）你這個賤貨。

　　　　（上官逢掙扎站起，被司徒德推出去）

邙赫拉：幹得好，你被雇用了。賞你一個元寶。（拿元寶給司徒

德）

（優丹上）

優　丹：您也賞個元寶給小人吧，大嬸。小人會教您一些常識。
　　　　仔細聽了——
　　　　　（數板）金玉滿堂不露白，
　　　　　　　　　學識淵博要裝呆。
　　　　　　　　　秤秤斤兩才放貸，
　　　　　　　　　騎馬勝過走路來。
　　　　　　　　　呼盧喝雉慎擲骰，
　　　　　　　　　輕信他人惹禍災。
　　　　　　　　　戒酒戒嫖家中待，
　　　　　　　　　自有好運發大財。

司徒德：這根本是廢話嘛，傻瓜。

優　丹：可不是？就像政客說的話嘛——空頭支票，不必兌現。
　　　　　（向邠赫拉）大嬸，「空頭」這玩意兒有用嗎？

邠赫拉：嘿，沒有啊，傻子。空頭就是一無所有。

優　丹：（向司徒德）請你告訴她，那就是她現在所有的。她是
　　　　不會相信傻瓜的。

邠赫拉：你這刻薄的傻瓜！

優　丹：大嬸，要不您請個人來教小人撒謊嘛。小人想學撒謊。

邠赫拉：你敢撒謊，看朕不抽你。

優　丹：唉，大嬸，不論小人撒不撒謊，都會挨鞭子啊。您看，
　　　　　（露出手肘）就連閉著嘴，公主都要抽我呢。傻瓜難為
　　　　唷。但小人可不要做您喔，您做的蠢事可比小人多得多

啦。

（都緒上）

邠赫拉：怎麼啦，緒兒？怎麼又皺眉啦？

優　丹：您以前不必在乎她皺眉，那時您算是個角兒。如今您只是個鴨蛋……

（看看都緒的臉色）哦，小人閉嘴就是。

（唱小調）閉嘴巴、閉嘴巴，

留下碎屑與殘渣。

只能瞪眼裝聾啞，

以免成為（指邠赫拉）大傻瓜。

都　緒：陛下，不僅您這個弄臣肆無忌憚，您那百名侍衛，也一樣傲慢無禮。動輒打鬧，惹是生非。您卻還包庇他們，令人無法忍受。為了維護宮內的安寧與秩序，必須懲戒他們。

優　丹：大嬸啊，豈不知——

（唱小調）麻雀餵養布穀鳥，

腦袋跟著也報銷。

邠赫拉：你還是朕的女兒麼？

都　緒：請您用點兒腦筋，不要耍脾氣。近來您愈發出格了。

優　丹：哇！車子拉馬，笨驢難道看不出來？

邠赫拉：你們認得朕麼？朕不是軒轅女皇麼？還要受你拘束？

優　丹：有名無實比無名無實還要糟哪。

邠赫拉：（故意）貴夫人，您是哪位？

都　緒：陛下，別裝傻，拜託！注意您的身分。既然年高，就該

　　　　德劭，有個穩重的樣子。您在府內毋須使喚百名侍衛，
　　　　請裁減隨員，不然女兒只好代勞了。

邪赫拉：（大喊）套馬，套馬，把朕的侍衛都叫過來。

　　　　（向都緒）你這賤人！朕不打擾你了。朕還有一個女兒。

都　緒：（冷冷地看著侍衛）沒規矩的暴徒！

邪赫拉：悔之晚矣！比起維兒，你是多麼——多麼——

　　　　啊，（敲打自己的腦袋）邪赫拉啊，邪赫拉，邪赫拉！

　　　　怎麼會失去理智，這般愚蠢呢！

　　　　（唱）想當初先皇逝大廈將傾，

　　　　　　　家國事亂如麻一肩擔承。

　　　　　　　年幼女在襁褓夜夜驚夢，

　　　　　　　忙撫慰暗落淚坐聽雞鳴。

都　緒：哎唷，這些個陳穀子、爛芝麻，提它作甚？

邪赫拉：（續唱）也曾經發號令操持權柄，

　　　　　　　　聖功頌萬國朝何等威風。

　　　　　　　　卻難料忤逆子忘恩負義，

　　　　　　　　到頭來全不念骨肉親情。

都　緒：陛下言重了。

邪赫拉：（續唱）小賤人施手段豺狼本性，

　　　　　　　　氣得我渾身顫老淚縱橫。

都　緒：您何必這麼衝動？

邪赫拉：（續唱）呼蒼天降災厄厲鬼報應，

　　　　　　　　南宮氏從今後斷子絕孫。

都　緒：呸呸呸！真是胡說。

邠赫拉：朕還有一個女兒。她一定會孝順朕，她會唾棄你。哼，
　　　　你等著瞧。

　　　　（邠赫拉怒下）

優　丹：大嬸，等等小人哪！

　　　　（優丹、司徒德和眾侍衛追下）

都　緒：瘋婆子！隨她去。

　　　　（上官逢上）

都　緒：如何？給二公主的信，寫好了麼？

上官逢：啟稟公主，早已寫好。

都　緒：快馬加鞭立即送去，不要誤了本宮的大事。

上官逢：遵命。（急下）

　　　　（南宮奧上）

南宮奧：（回首張望）這倒怪了！

　　　　（向都緒）公主，適才本宮撞見陛下，正待請安，誰知
　　　　她卻不予理會，怒氣沖沖地逕自離去了。不知發生何事？

都　緒：噢，小事一樁，不勞駙馬掛懷。

南宮奧：公主，陛下即使退位了，也還是皇娘。於情於理，我們
　　　　都應敬她三分。

都　緒：哼，本宮自有道理，駙馬不必說教。

南宮奧：這……

都　緒：（旁白）本宮倒要看看，你能倔到幾時？哼！

　　　　（切光）

第四場　計陷

（端木府邸）

（端木蒙緩步上）

端木蒙：二公主和夏侯駙馬今晚竟要光臨寒舍？(眼珠一轉)哈！
　　　　這敢情好。我導的這齣大戲，正好缺少兩個龍套。

　　　　（向樓上喊）

　　　　大哥，小弟有要事相告。請快下來。

　　　　（端木加出現，下樓，端木蒙迎上）

　　　　夏侯駙馬得到密報，有人告你謀反，他正匆忙趕來。

端木加：（大吃一驚）哪有此事？這、這是從何說起？

端木蒙：爹爹盯著你呢。大哥，快逃。

　　　　啊，爹爹來了。對不住，小弟得做個樣子。（拔劍）拔
　　　　劍哪，假裝自衛，認真打。（端木加拔劍）對，就是這
　　　　樣。（兩人過招，大聲）快投降，跟我見爹爹去。——
　　　　喂，拿火把來呦！——（小聲）快逃，大哥，往東邊。
　　　　——（大聲）火把，火把！——（小聲）好，保重。

　　　　（端木加下）

　　　　（自語）我得流點兒血，（自刺手臂）這樣更容易哄人。
　　　　——（大聲）爹爹，爹爹！——住手，住手！救命啊！

　　　　（端木格和眾侍衛持火把衝上）

端木格：阿蒙，沒事吧？那個壞胚子呢？

端木蒙：爹爹，您瞧，孩兒受傷了。他躲在暗處行刺我。

端木格：可惡，他在哪裡？你傷得如何？

端木蒙：沒有大礙。但請爹爹小心，他想謀刺您呢！

端木格：他在哪裡？

端木蒙：他朝西邊逃了。

端木格：追！

　　　　（眾侍衛下）

端木蒙：爹爹，孩兒拒絕與他同謀，還斥責他泯滅天良，不想他就偷襲我。

端木格：哼，這個大逆不道的畜牲！老夫今晚即刻稟明公主和駙馬，對他發出格殺令。一旦發現他的蹤跡，就地處斬。

端木蒙：爹爹，孩兒極力勸阻，他卻一意孤行。還大言不慚地說，不怕被揭發。因為孩兒只是一個雜種，沒有人會相信我。

端木格：哼，殺千刀的畜牲！還妄想否認自己的罪行？好孩子，為父做主，定會讓你繼承端木氏的名位與爵祿。

　　　　（一侍衛上）

侍　　衛：稟大人，二公主、夏侯駙馬駕到。

端木格：快快出迎。

　　　　（眾侍衛列隊上，夏侯康、都紹隨上，端木格、端木蒙迎上）

端木格、端木蒙：參見公主、駙馬。

夏侯康、都紹：免禮。

　　　　（眾人入府，分別就座）

夏侯康：端木大人，令公子怎麼受傷了？

端木格：啊，微臣真是痛心疾首啊。

都　紹：如此說來，傳聞不假？端木加當真預謀弒親？

端木格：家門不幸啊，慚愧！

夏侯康：端木蒙，本宮聽說你善盡了孝道。

端木蒙：不敢，小子但盡本分而已。

端木格：他不僅揭發這個惡毒的陰謀，還為了逮捕孽子而受傷。

夏侯康：好。立即發出緝捕令，布下天羅地網，一定要將他斬首
　　　　示眾，以儆效尤。

端木格：多謝駙馬。

都　紹：（以目睇之，含笑）端木蒙，你是好樣兒的。本宮很欣
　　　　賞你的孝心。孝子必是忠臣。現在就任命你為侍衛統領，
　　　　供奉內廷如何？

夏侯康：如此甚好。

端木蒙：多謝公主，多謝駙馬，屬下必忠心事主，萬死不辭。

端木格：多謝提拔。

都　紹：端木大人，深夜打擾，真是過意不去。但事出緊急，必
　　　　須相商。

端木格：是，微臣願聞其詳。

都　紹：大公主遣人來報，陛下已經離開。若她待會兒來了，你
　　　　就說本宮身體不適，早已安寢。

端木格：這個……不妥吧？

夏侯康：你聽命行事，不必多言。

　　　　（一侍衛上）

侍　衛：報，陛下駕到。

（都紹、夏侯康打個手勢，下。眾侍衛隨下）

（邡赫拉、司徒德改扮為公孫凱、優丹、眾侍衛上）
（端木格、端木蒙迎上）

端木格：不知陛下駕到，未曾遠迎，尚乞恕罪。陛下請。

　　　　（眾人入府）

邡赫拉：端木大人，朕剛去二公主那裡，聽說公主和駙馬忽然來
　　　　此。慈母正等著愛女的服侍，他們人呢？

端木格：公主有些頭疼……

邡赫拉：頭疼？朕才頭疼得厲害呢！——不，別急，或許紹兒真
　　　　是玉體微恙。

　　　　（旁白）忍耐些吧，可別衝動。

優　丹：大嬸，您很快就會看到另一個女兒有多麼貼心！

邡赫拉：怎麼講？

優　丹：酸蘋果就是酸蘋果。除非基因改造，要不怎麼也甜不了。

邡赫拉：你是說——？

優　丹：您知道為什麼人會有五官麼？

邡赫拉：朕——不知。

優　丹：嘿，因為要「眼觀四面，耳聽八方」嘛。就算是無味無
　　　　嗅的東西，也可以仔細分辨啦。

邡赫拉：朕——錯待她了。

優　丹：大嬸，您知道蚵仔如何造自己的殼麼？

　　　　（邡赫拉緩緩搖頭）

　　　　小人也不知。但小人知道蝸牛為什麼要背房子。

邠赫拉：為了什麼？

優　丹：嘿，好把頭放進去啊。不是為了送給女兒，害自己的觸
　　　　角沒個匣子擺。

邠赫拉：你……

（夏侯康、都紹上）

夏侯康：參見陛下。

都　紹：陛下安康。

邠赫拉：啊，紹兒，你大姐真不是個東西！著實令朕痛心。

都　紹：陛下息怒，想是您誤會了大姐。

邠赫拉：哦？此話怎講？

都　紹：大姐的孝心，無人不知。如她合理約束您那些鬧事的侍
　　　　衛，又怎能責怪於她？

邠赫拉：她是個賤貨！——咦，你哪兒來的消息？

都　紹：這您就甭管了。陛下啊，您老了。雖然來日無多，總是
　　　　這麼顛三倒四也不成。依女兒之見哪——

邠赫拉：怎麼樣？

都　紹：您還是回去向大姐說句好話，就當您錯怪了她。

邠赫拉：求她寬恕？如此這般？（下跪，司徒德忙扶她起來）真
　　　　是成何體統！

都　紹：陛下，您這才是成何體統！俗話說得好：「忍片時風平
　　　　浪靜，退一步海闊天空」，您又何苦跟自己過不去呢？

邠赫拉：哼！朕絕不回去。她要裁減朕一半的隨扈。像她這般忘
　　　　恩負義，朕詛咒她遭天打雷劈，下十八層地獄……

夏侯康：這是何言語？

邙赫拉：上刀山、下油鍋、挖眼拔舌、剖腹洗腸、全身長滿爛疥
　　　　瘡！

都　紹：哎唷，天哪，您怎麼這般口不擇言？您發怒時也會如此
　　　　咒罵我麼？

邙赫拉：不，紹兒，朕絕不會咒罵你。你是個溫柔孝順的好女兒，
　　　　你不會剝奪朕的享受，裁減朕的隨扈，甚至把朕關在門
　　　　外。你不會忘記是誰賜給你這大好江山的吧？

優　丹：（旁白）大雁朝南飛，冬至接大寒啦。

　　　　（唱小調）爹娘有錢是個寶，

　　　　　　　　　噓寒問暖烹佳餚。

　　　　　　　　　爹娘沒錢當雜草，

　　　　　　　　　三餐茶飯少鍋瓢。

　　　　　　　　　八字生來已顛倒，

　　　　　　　　　何必辛苦走一遭？

都　紹：陛下，咱們還是打開天窗說亮話吧——

　　　　（一侍衛領上官逢上）

上官逢：啟稟公主，大公主駕到。

都　紹：啊，大姐果然來了。（欣喜迎上）

　　　　（都緒上）

邙赫拉：（向都緒）你有何臉面來見朕？

　　　　（都紹、都緒親熱牽手）

　　　　噢，紹兒，你竟和這賤人勾搭？

都　緒：陛下，女兒有何過失，值得您說得這麼難聽？

邖赫拉：不孝的賤人，活活氣死我了！

都　紹：我勸您還是跟著大姐回去吧，陛下啊——

　　　　（唱）年事已高要服老，

　　　　　　　切莫任性太張狂。

　　　　　　　姐妹輪流來奉養，

　　　　　　　裁幾個奴才有何妨？

邖赫拉：不——

　　　　（唱）萬壽分疆有協議，

　　　　　　　紹兒此言忒無良。

　　　　　　　縱然飢寒把命喪，

　　　　　　　絕不低頭（指都緒）向豺狼。

都　緒：哦？——

　　　　（唱）百名侍衛亂無章，

　　　　　　　整飭家規理應當。

　　　　　　　去留且由您細想，

　　　　　　　多言無益說分疆。

邖赫拉：天哪，朕怎麼會生出你這種女兒？好個「孝順皇娘情意
　　　　真」！

　　　　（唱）冷酷無情一魍魎，

　　　　　　　鐵石鑄就歹心腸。

　　　　　　　孝順是你親口講，

　　　　　　　斤斤計較忘倫常。

　　　　　　　但願你悔過知禮讓，

　　　　　　　也不枉咱母女這一場。

（白）朕不再打擾你了。我們就此永別，不再相見。朕和百名侍衛可以長住紹兒的宮殿。

都　紹：且慢，陛下，您誤會了。女兒尚未準備就緒，這會兒也不便接待您。您還是聽大姐的吧。

邠赫拉：這可是真心話？

都　紹：是啊。陛下，五十個侍衛不是很好麼？您要那麼多隨扈幹嘛呢？徒然製造麻煩。

都　緒：陛下，您何不就讓她的人，或我的人，來侍候您？

都　紹：這樣很好啊。陛下，若是他們有所怠慢，我們也好管教。下月來訪，請您最多就帶二十五人吧。多餘的侍衛，女兒可不能收留。

邠赫拉：朕把一切都給了你們……

都　緒：給得正是時候。

邠赫拉：二十五人？紹兒，這是你說的？

都　紹：是的，陛下，不能更多。

邠赫拉：（向都緒）那朕跟你回去。你那五十人是她的雙分，你比她孝順兩倍。

都　緒：陛下，其實您何必要二十五個，或十個、五個跟班？宮內人手足以供您使喚了。

都　紹：大姐說的是，一個都嫌多餘。

邠赫拉：住口！你們——你們這兩個狼心狗肺的東西，竟敢提起「多餘」二字——

　　　　（唱）片瓦覆頂避風寒，

　　　　　　　何須藻井飾玉環？

　　　　粗衣大布裹身暖，

　　　　何須雲錦繡斑斕？

　　　　縱然是乞丐落魄卑田院，

　　　　隨身也有幾件破衣衫。

　　　　倘若伊孑然一身無餘物，

　　　　且問人間——何處覓清歡？

　　（白）天哪！這叫「念念牽引骨肉情」？「直取明月星」才真是多餘！看看這兩個禽獸是如何對待他們的老皇娘！（陷入瘋狂）天地有靈，一定要嚴懲這些叛徒！

　　（遠處傳來轟隆雷聲，隨之雨聲嘩啦）

　　天哪！天哪！你一定要讓朕痛心而亡麼？

　　（邔赫拉衝下，端木格、司徒德、優丹及眾侍衛追下）

夏侯康：（看看門外）這風暴來勢不小啊。

都　紹：這府邸小，老太婆和她那幫人不便安頓。

都　緒：這要怪她自己。愚蠢又固執，就只能落到這種下場。

都　紹：若只有她一個人，本宮倒是樂於招呼。其他侍衛可不行。

都　緒：本宮也是這麼想。

　　（端木格上）

端木格：陛下大發雷霆。

夏侯康：她待如何？

端木格：陛下叫人備馬，不知要前往何處？

夏侯康：隨她去。

都　緒：是呀，愛去哪兒去哪兒。大人，千萬不許挽留她。

端木格：哎呀，可這天快黑了，狂風四起，方圓十里連棵樹都沒

有啊。

都　紹：大人，這任性之人哪，自討苦吃，合該得個教訓。

夏侯康：正是。大人，還是關好門戶，小心風暴為是。

　　　　（都緒、都紹眼神交換，會心一笑，攜手下。眾隨下。
　　　　端木格、端木蒙留在場上）

端木格：不近人情，阿蒙。他們竟然如此對待陛下，豈有此理！

端木蒙：蠻橫無理，莫此為甚。

端木格：吔！且莫聲張。（看看左右，低聲）為父剛收到一封密
　　　　函，已鎖進箱子裡。你等著吧，不出三日，赫連軍就會
　　　　抵達。我等要忠於陛下。老夫現在去找陛下，以確保她
　　　　的安全。你去敷衍公主和駙馬，不要讓他們察覺老夫的
　　　　計畫。

端木蒙：是。

端木格：阿蒙，小心！（匆匆下）

端木蒙：哼，愛獻殷勤的蠢老頭！哈哈！（奸笑）

　　　　（唱）自作聰明匹夫勇，

　　　　　　　誡令只當耳邊風。

　　　　　　　將計就計假唬弄，

　　　　　　　且看大爺我——領賞立大功。

（切光）

〔中場休息〕

第五場　風暴

（曠野）

（環形投影：寂靜黑夜，雷電交加，風雨不已，寒意四起）

【幕後伴唱】：日月星辰黯無光，

天地失序不尋常。

倫理乖違情義喪，

國事從此問蜩螗。

邠赫拉：（內唱）率剌剌冷冽刺骨暴風狂，

（邠赫拉上，優丹隨上）

（接唱）嘩啦啦大雨傾盆淹汪洋。

撥不開層層疊疊雲霧障，

分不清水花淚花視茫茫。

優　丹：大嬸，去奉承公主兩句好話吧。躲進暖屋裡，總強過這麼吹風淋雨。

邠赫拉：（似未聽聞，續唱）渾不知世態炎涼道德喪，

欠隄防諂媚小人正當行。

可嘆我神智昏亂心血淌，

無奈何白髮蒼蒼痛斷腸。

【畫外音】：（漸強）女兒不孝！女兒不孝！女兒不孝！女兒不孝！女兒不孝！女兒不孝！……

邪赫拉：（續唱，爆發）恨不得咒詛雷霆從天降，

　　　　　　　　　　鬧一場生靈覆滅同遭殃。

優　丹：大嬸，頭殼沒壞的，都知道要回去。

邪赫拉：不，朕絕不回去！這風雨難道是衝著朕來的麼？（仰頭
　　　　視天）你們要做卑鄙的幫兇，一起來為難朕麼？哈哈！
　　　　不、不，朕——朕禁受得住。傻瓜啊，儘管來吧。

優　丹：這時候還逞強的，才真是傻瓜。風雨可不會管什麼好人
　　　　壞人的……

邪赫拉：（向天大喊）有本事就去對付那些沒心沒肝的畜牲吧！
　　　　（唱）怒火起地裂天崩轟隆響，

　　　　　　　　劈開這萬惡淵藪振乾綱。

　　　　　　　　驀然裡懲凶誅惡起風暴，

　　　　　　　　管教他偽善邪佞無處藏。

　　　　　　　　且莫要揚威耀武朕頭上，

　　　　　　　　欺善怕惡、不是好兒郎！

　　　　（司徒德改扮為公孫凱上）

司徒德：（一路張望，大聲）陛下，陛下……

優　丹：（揮舞雙手）這裡、在這裡！

司徒德：天哪，陛下，屬下可找到您了。這等可怕的天氣，折騰
　　　　人哪。

優　丹：早說了唄。

司徒德：陛下，附近有個小茅舍，可以暫避風雨。請您稍作安歇，
　　　　屬下再去找公主討個公道。

邪赫拉：朕好累啊！腦子不管用了，一片混亂……

優　丹：大嬸，「留得青山在，不怕沒柴燒」，咱們先去茅舍吧。

邨赫拉：不錯，孩子。（向司徒德）朋友，帶我們去茅舍吧。

司徒德：陛下請。

　　　　（司徒德前導，眾人轉場，至茅舍前）

司徒德：陛下，快進去吧。

邨赫拉：別管朕。

司徒德：陛下，請進去吧。風雨正大著呢。

邨赫拉：這種狂風暴雨，對朕來說，真算不得什麼。朕所感受的
　　　　風暴，可比這個嚴重多了。朕的心都碎了！噢，緒兒、
　　　　紹兒，竟在這種夜晚把老身關在門外？慷慨的老媽媽賜
　　　　給了你們一切……啊，不能再這麼想，我受不了！太痛
　　　　心了！（踉蹌）

司徒德：（搶上扶住）陛下，請進去吧。

邨赫拉：嗯。（邁出一步，止步，看優丹）小子，冷嗎？
　　　　（優丹發抖，點頭）
　　　　朕也好冷啊。可憐的小子！你先進去吧。
　　　　（優丹入屋，司徒德扶邨赫拉隨後）

優　丹：（四處摸索）好黑啊，伸手不見五指，這裡有些稻草。
　　　　（開始鋪墊）

邨赫拉：（有感而發）這般天氣，那些無家可歸的窮人呵——
　　　　（唱）衣衫襤褸不蔽體，
　　　　　　　飢寒交迫無所依。
　　　　　　　老身淪落一至此，
　　　　　　　愧悔昔日不自知。

　　　　　寄語顯貴施賑濟，

　　　　　公道昭然本於茲。

優　丹：（摸到端木加，尖叫）哇，有鬼啊！（躲到邠赫拉身後）

司徒德：怎麼啦？

優　丹：（哆嗦）那裡，有鬼！

司徒德：（上前）什麼東西？出來！

　　　　　（端木加喬裝成瘋頭陀上）

端木加：（手舞足蹈）波羅波若摩訶薩，迦葉須菩提！

司徒德：原來是個頭陀。

端木加：去，急急如律令！妖魔棄五欲，穢惡便滅，鬼怪布施無
　　　　　量。

司徒德：滿口瘋言瘋語，不知講些什麼？

邠赫拉：你也把一切都給了女兒麼？

端木加：一缽食，善知識，行行好。老衲餓了兩天，只啃了一隻
　　　　　壁虎。好冷啊。

邠赫拉：你什麼都沒留下？全部給了她們？唉，願你的女兒被天
　　　　　雷轟破腦門！

司徒德：陛下，頭陀沒有女兒。

邠赫拉：殺千刀的叛徒！如非不孝之女，誰能這樣侮辱他、折磨
　　　　　他？

端木加：小心邪魔歪道，頭陀好冷。

邠赫拉：可憐的人，善待他吧。這些都是身外之物，留著無益，
　　　　　捨了吧！（動手去扯自己的外衣，端木加竄向門口）

優　丹：大嬸，別生氣，這種夜晚不宜——裸奔。

　　　　（端木格持火把、行囊上，撞到端木加）

端木格：你是何人？

端木加：啊——（認出其父，忙閃躲，口裡喃喃）善知識穿著破
　　　　芒鞋，吞食蠑螈、死老鼠……（避於牆隅）

端木格：（搖搖頭）一個瘋頭陀！

司徒德：（迎上）陛下在此。

端木格：（向邲赫拉）老臣叩見陛下。

邲赫拉：你是——蓬萊方士？

端木格：陛下，老臣端木格啊。雖然子女喪盡天良，視父母如草
　　　　芥，老臣也不能昧著良心。無論如何，都要顧及忠義。
　　　　（解下行囊，交給司徒德）這裡有些乾糧、衣物，權且
　　　　收下。老臣已備妥車馬，請陛下移駕至安全之處。

邲赫拉：（拉住優丹）咱們來占卜吉凶，看看禍福……（走開）

司徒德：（向端木格）大人，您瞧見了，陛下神智不清了。

端木格：唉，怪不得她。公主置陛下於不顧，司徒大人的擔心果
　　　　然不錯。其實老夫自個兒也不好受……老夫也有個逆
　　　　子，近日差一點兒就要了老夫的命。真令人痛心！

司徒德：大人保重。眼下還是先安頓陛下吧。

端木格：嗯。（走向邲赫拉）陛下、陛下，請隨老臣來。

　　　　（端木格拉著邲赫拉，邲赫拉拉著優丹下，司徒德隨下）

端木加：（上前，拍胸）幸好不曾識破。只是這——
　　　　（唱）陛下落難事有詐，

　　　　　　　緝捕嚴查父疑咱。

　　　　　　　苟全性命擔驚怕，

（怒而擊拳）痛恨小人罪名加。

（白）唉！

（續唱）繁華如夢且作罷，

　　　　裝瘋賣傻度生涯。

　　　　假作真時真亦假，

（白）忍飢受凍、托缽苦行，靜待他日——

（續唱）眼瞪眼來牙還牙。

（切光）

第六場　剜目

（端木府邸）
（夏侯康讀信，都緒、都紹在旁，端木蒙侍立在側）

夏侯康：（讀信）哼，這個吃裡扒外的老傢伙！可見令兄要取他
性命亦非心狠手辣，都怪他咎由自取。

端木蒙：駙馬爺啊——
（唱）不意他是心腹患，
　　　　勾結外邦犯軒轅。
　　　　大義滅親非所願，
　　　　忠孝今朝難兩全。
　　　　時人議論方寸亂，
　　　　姑息只能養權奸。
　　　　直面上報速查辦，
　　　　殺雞儆猴趁風帆。

夏侯康：難得你如此忠心，本宮會查個清楚。（持信予都緒，都
緒讀信）先擢升你為將軍，日後還有重賞。

端木蒙：謝駙馬。（故作姿態）不過——
（續唱）也憐老父糊塗犯，
　　　　　還望駙馬量刑寬。

夏侯康：嗯。（看端木蒙一眼）好個孝子！
來人哪！去把端木格這個叛徒抓來見本宮。

（侍衛乙承應，下）

夏侯康：大姐，事不宜遲，請您起駕回宮。赫連軍即將入侵，端
　　　　木格就是內應，我們得準備迎敵。

都　紹：立即吊死這個老賊。

都　緒：（把信交還夏侯康）把他的眼珠子挖出來。

夏侯康：放心，本宮自會定奪。

　　　　（向端木蒙）端木將軍，本宮派你護送大公主，即刻出
　　　　發。

都　紹：（瞟了端木蒙、都緒一眼，欲攔阻）這……這不妥吧？

都　緒：有何不妥？也免得端木將軍在此目睹審訊，多有不便。

都　紹：那……那將軍可要儘速趕回，此刻正是用人之際。

端木蒙：末將遵命。

都　緒：備馬。

　　　　（一侍衛承應，下）

　　　　咱們分頭行事。

　　　　（都緒、端木蒙下）

　　　　（侍衛乙帶端木格上）

侍衛乙：啟稟駙馬，人犯帶到。

夏侯康：哼，上刑！

　　　　（眾侍衛把端木格縛在刑架上）

端木格：幹什麼？這是幹什麼？怎麼回事？

都　紹：狡獪的賣國賊，還要裝蒜！

夏侯康：端木格，事到如今，你有何話說？

端木格：請駙馬明示，老臣何錯之有？

都　紹：唷，嘖嘖嘖，這死鴨子的嘴倒挺硬的！看來是不打不招。
　　　　先打他四十大板！

眾侍衛：（打端木格，端木格痛喊呼冤）一十！二十！三十！四
　　　　十！

端木格：冤枉啊！

夏侯康：冤枉？哼，（亮信）此信即是鐵證。你是如何勾結赫連
　　　　國的？說！

端木格：小公主不日回國省親，怎能算是勾結？

夏侯康：狡辯。

都　紹：信口胡言。

夏侯康：你把陛下弄到哪裡去了？

　　　　（端木格不言語）

都　紹：說啊，死老賊！

端木格：哼！——

　　　　（唱）暴雨狂風路途險，

　　　　　　　曠野無垠徹骨寒。

　　　　　　　忍見陛下魂魄散，

　　　　　　　連夜送她到邊關。

　　　　　　　骨肉親情不可斷，

　　　　　　　百善原以孝為先。

　　　　　　　罔顧人倫遭天譴，

　　　　　　　老夫拭目——等著看。

夏侯康：老匹夫，你絕對看不到——本宮現在就親自挖出你的雙
　　　　眼，踩扁這對眼珠子！

（拔出小刀）抓緊他！（眾侍衛按住端木格）

端木格： 你們還是不是人哪？……

　　　　（夏侯康動手剜出一目，端木格慘叫）救命啊！天哪！

都　紹： 這邊會嘲笑那邊，還有一隻。

夏侯康：（獰笑）何謂天譴？此之謂也！（欲剜另一目）

侍衛乙：（阻擋）住手，駙馬，請住手。太殘忍了。

都　紹： 你這狗崽子敢抗命？

夏侯康： 不怕死的狗奴才！

　　　　（夏侯康拔劍刺侍衛乙，後者閃過，亦拔劍刺中夏侯康）

都　紹： 來人，把他抓起來！

　　　　（眾侍衛抓住侍衛乙）

侍衛乙：（向端木格）大人，您還有一眼，可以看到他受傷的報應。

　　　　（都紹取劍刺死侍衛乙）

夏侯康：（忍痛）才不讓它看到什麼。出來，髒肉凍！（剜出另一目）

端木格：（慘叫）天哪！阿蒙，你在哪裡？你看到了麼？你要為老父報仇啊！

都　紹： 去你的，奸賊！阿蒙才不會同情你咧。正是他大義滅親，呈報你的通敵行徑。

端木格： 啊——是他？（頹然）這麼說來，阿加也是被這逆子陷害的了……

都　紹： 把他推出門外，讓他自生自滅。

　　　　（眾侍衛推出端木格）

　　（夏侯康踉蹌，發出呻吟聲）

　　駙馬，（上前攙扶）還好麼？

夏侯康：（虛弱）本宮受傷不輕，快叫……太醫。

　　（一侍衛承應，下）

都　紹：駙馬小心。

　　（二人同下）

　　（切光）

第七場　孽緣

（表演區 A：都緒宮殿。表演區 B：端木府邸）

（表演區 A）
（都緒、南宮奧交談中）

（侍衛丙上）

侍衛丙：報，赫連軍已然挺進我國邊境。

南宮奧：知道了。（揮手，侍衛丙下）唉，赫連軍逼近，本應迎
　　　　　敵。但領軍者是小妹，打的又是勤王救母的旗號，教人
　　　　　好生為難！

都　緒：駙馬，咱們得趕緊拿個主意啊。

南宮奧：這……

　　　　　（上官逢上）

　　　　　二公主那邊有何消息？

上官逢：稟駙馬，夏侯駙馬被自己的侍衛刺殺身亡了。

都　緒：（一驚）當真？

南宮奧：可是兵變？

上官逢：不是。夏侯駙馬正對叛賊端木格施刑，剜其眼珠，有一
　　　　　侍衛勸阻不成，拔劍刺殺了駙馬。

南宮奧：什麼？剜其眼珠？端木大人忠心事主，卻有這等遭遇，
　　　　　真是駭人聽聞。他瞎了一眼麼？

上官逢：雙眼。那侍衛立即被誅殺，端木格也被逐了出去。

南宮奧：而今二妹夫身亡，可見「舉頭三尺有神明」，報應來得
　　　　好快呀。只是端木大人他……

都　緒：駙馬，情況緊急，還不快去備戰！淨在這裡囉唆什麼？

南宮奧：公主怎麼這般說話？凡事抬不過個「理」字，二妹夫痛
　　　　下殺手，原是過分了……

都　緒：好了，駙馬，先去備戰吧。回頭有了閒工夫，再來說三
　　　　道四。

南宮奧：唉，兩國交戰，苦了百姓！（下）

都　緒：這個窩囊廢，一點兒魄力也沒有。哪裡比得上阿蒙，氣
　　　　宇軒昂又聰明幹練……（微笑）這一路之上，更是體貼
　　　　周到。（轉念）啊，不妙，現今二妹守寡，這調兵遣將……
　　　　（尋思）他倆孤男寡女，共處一室，同心禦敵，難保不
　　　　日久生情。萬一阿蒙被那賤人拐去了，可不就辜負了本
　　　　宮這番心意？不成，本宮得想個一勞永逸的法子……（琢
　　　　磨著）啊，有了！（提筆寫信）

　　　　（旁唱）金枝玉葉自主張，

　　　　　　　　烏鴉豈可配鳳凰？

　　　　　　　　信誓旦旦君莫忘，

　　　　　　　　天生一對世無雙。

　　　　　　　　大鵬扶搖青雲上，

　　　　　　　　吩咐情郎放眼量。

　　　　　　　　斬草除根布羅網，

　　　　　　　　軒轅版圖永同享。

（封信，白）總管，立即出發，（交信）這封密函務必
親交端木將軍。本宮要他照章行事。

上官逢：遵命。（欲下）

都　緒：回來！

上官逢：（止步）公主有何交代？

都　緒：讓端木格這瞎眼老賊在外遊蕩，恐怕眾口悠悠，委實不
妥。去張貼告示，懸賞捕殺。

上官逢：是。（下）

都　緒：（得意地笑）二妹呀，二妹，「人不為己，天誅地滅」。
可別怨我心狠手辣！

（表演區 A 燈漸弱，表演區 B 燈漸強）

（表演區 B）

（都紹、端木蒙上）

都　紹：（嫵媚）將軍，你是知道的——

（唱）駙馬不幸以身殉，

　　　　國政殷憂萬緒紛。

　　　　廟堂既要千里駿，

　　　　後宮還缺知心人。

端木蒙：呀——

（旁唱）莫非交了桃花運，

　　　　琵琶弦外是何音？

都　紹：（肢體挑逗，續唱）紅燭帳暖春宵恨，

夜夜無眠暗沉吟。

端木蒙：（續旁唱）箇中似有難言隱，

公主果然情意深。

都　紹：（取杯酒遞上，續唱）合歡美酒及時飲，

君須憐我我憐君。

端木蒙：（接過酒杯，續旁唱）且待今宵共鴛枕，

輕易錦鯉躍龍門。

（一口飲盡，白）蒙公主垂青，末將敢不盡力！哈哈！

都　紹：（叮嚀）將軍，可不能辜負本宮。

端木蒙：公主放心，末將定效──微軀之勞。

都　紹：（忽然想起，認真）阿蒙，你和大公主之間無有什麼吧？

端木蒙：（掩飾）什麼？和大公主？哦──當然無有。

都　紹：這就好。本宮可不能容忍……

端木蒙：公主多心了。

都　紹：天色不早，你……

端木蒙：末將隨後就來。

（都紹媚笑下）

端木蒙：（攤手）兩位公主都對我有意，這要如何是好？

（唱）先後許下千金諾，

魚與熊掌難兼得。

兩宮勢力非小可，

機巧可別弄成拙。

風雲多變心有數，

知是悲歡抑離合？

隔岸暫且先觀火，
金蟬終究能脫殼。

（切光）

第八場　重圓

（曠野）
（端木格拄杖上）

端木格：（跌跌撞撞，摸索前行）蒼天哪——
　　　　（唱）逆子他巧逢迎背地暗算，
　　　　　　　暮年人悲悽悽慘絕人寰。
　　　　　　　渾噩噩明眼人卻似無眼，
　　　　　　　全不察阿蒙他詭計多端。
　　　　　　　茫茫然無路走悔之已晚，
　　　　　　　可笑我失雙目洞察其奸。
　　　　　　　恨只恨忒寵溺心存偏見，
　　　　　　　思加兒淚縱橫愁恨頻添。
　　　　　　　蒼天哪蒼天，何時才開眼？
　　　　　　　善惡終有報，父子兩團圓。

（端木加喬裝成瘋頭陀上）

端木加：（旁白）呀，來人似是爹爹？（閃躲一旁）可怎生搖搖
　　　晃晃？

端木格：（咬牙切齒）這個殺千刀的畜牲！沒天良的逆子啊！

端木加：（旁白）呀——
　　　　（旁唱）見此景不由我心驚膽戰，

爹爹他咬牙根罵聲連連。

我只能暗垂淚百口莫辯，

恨奸人兩面刀巧進讒言。

端木格：（察覺有人）有人麼？是哪個？不要欺負老瞎子！

端木加：（旁白）什麼？他瞎了？我原以為命運已悲慘至極，孰料世道反覆，一至於斯！爹爹他——

（續旁唱）卻不知何故忽遭劫難，

竟落得孤伶伶舉步維艱。

端木格：到底是哪個？

端木加：（續旁唱）我本待迎上前父子相見，

（上前兩步，退後，旁白）不——

（續旁唱）且偽裝莫現身以策安全。

（白）嘻嘻，瘋頭陀三缽一衣要袈裟。南無摩訶薩，無住布施囉。

端木格：原來是瘋頭陀，風雨之夜見過。老夫還以為……

端木加：以為什麼？

端木格：唉，無有什麼。昔日老夫總是自以為是，有眼不會看，有耳不會聽，才落得今朝如此淒涼。原來人生亦如戲，世事本無常啊。

端木加：（旁白）此話教人好不明白。爹爹這般模樣，眼眸還淌著鮮血呢，我真是演不下去！

端木格：「天地不仁，以萬物為芻狗」，老夫這回當真領教了。

端木加：（旁白）但還是要勉為其難，繼續扮演啊。

（白）喂，善知識，你要去哪裡？

端木格：老夫要去邊關。你認得路麼？可以引領老夫麼？

端木加：哈，怎麼不認得？不拘什麼康莊大道、羊腸小徑，九拐
　　　　十八彎，都是頭陀走慣了的。只是——嘻嘻，瘋子引著
　　　　瞎子走，你放心麼？

端木格：這有何妨？現今世道正是如此。橫豎老夫走投無路，到
　　　　哪裡都是一樣的。

端木加：好啊，善知識，（伸手拉端木格）隨我來。

端木格：有勞了。

　　　　（二人圓場，以示行路，或可作翻山渡河之身段）

【幕後伴唱】：父子相見不相認，

　　　　　　　　各含血淚吞苦辛。

端木加：（旁白）但見他——

　　　　（旁唱）眼眸空洞長吁嘆，

　　　　　　　　血漬斑斑猶未乾。

　　　　　　　　山高水低天昏暗，

　　　　　　　　扎掙向前步蹣跚。

　　　　　　　　究竟如何忍心探，

　　　　　　　　套問爹爹吐真言。

　　　　（白）善知識啊——

　　　　（唱）行路難、行路難，

　　　　　　　因何千里去邊關？

端木格：唉，頭陀有所不知，老夫呵——

　　　　（續唱）一時不察失雙眼，

　　　　　　忠心竟然受顛連。

　　　　　　討伐叛逆秉公斷，

　　　　　　面陳王后在赫連。

　　　　　　拚卻殘軀向前趲，

　　　　　　辨奸何懼行路難！

端木加：　（續唱）何人搆陷失雙眼？

　　　　　　　　　何人累你受顛連？

端木格：　（續唱）未防阿蒙設計陷，

　　　　　　　　　委屈加兒受熬煎。

　　　　　　　　　老夫愚昧遭蒙騙，

　　　　　　　　　父子雙雙含屈冤。

端木加：　（續旁唱，大驚）可恨小人忒陰險，

　　　　　　　　　　　原來阿蒙——阿蒙是內奸！

　　　　　　　　　　機關算盡情義斷，

　　　　　（憤怒）從今骨肉不周全！

端木格：　（續唱）今日恍然已嫌晚，

　　　　　　　　　回首前塵愧無言。

　　　　　　　　　雙袖龍鍾徒掩面，

　　　　　（痛哭）思念加兒淚不乾。

端木加：　（續旁唱）爹爹悲哭仰天嘆，

　　　　　　　　　　真情流露碎心肝。

　　　　　　　　　不禁落淚上前喚——

　　　　　（白）啊，爹爹！

　　　　　（續唱）孩兒跪地來請安！

端木格：你……你是加兒？

端木加：正是孩兒！

端木格：加兒，加兒！爹爹錯怪你了！（撫摸其臉；父子相擁而
泣）真的是你麼？

端木加：是的。孩兒偽裝成瘋頭陀，以避人耳目。

端木格：蒼天畢竟有眼，能活著相見，老夫死而無憾了。

端木加：爹爹別說這不吉利的話，請放寬心。孩兒相信，冤屈定
能昭雪，否極總會泰來。

（端木格一個踉蹌）

（搶上攙扶）爹爹小心！

（二人續走小半個圓場）

【幕後伴唱】：父子相見終相認，

亦步亦趨心連心、心連心。

（上官逢上）

上官逢：小人奉大公主之命，前來送信給端木將軍。這一路之上，
連個人影也沒瞧見。呀，且慢，前方來的——可不是懸
賞捕殺的瞎眼老賊麼？（亮劍）哈哈，真是天助我也。
（上前要殺端木格）難怪眼皮跳，原是好運到。此時要
發財，誰也擋不掉！

端木加：住手。（以隨身棍格擋）

上官逢：滾開，臭頭陀！別礙著老爺的好事。

端木加：不准你欺侮老人家！

（二人開打。混亂中，端木格跌坐在地）

上官逢： 這身手？你不是頭陀！（細看）你是端木……
　　　　（端木加搶過劍來，刺殺上官）

上官逢： 啊！——那這信……（斷氣）

端木加： （上前扶起端木格）爹爹受驚了！
　　　　爹爹暫且歇息片刻，（扶端木格坐石上）孩兒先把這個
　　　　惡棍藏起來，以免旁人發覺。（拉扯上官逢，發現信）
　　　　啊，未料這惡棍竟是信差。（拆信閱讀，大驚）這是——
　　　　——給阿蒙的信？嗯，我且收好，日後或有大用。（收信，
　　　　拖上官逢下）

　　　　（邠赫拉頭戴野草、披頭散髮上）

邠赫拉： （對著一排石頭）朕乃軒轅女皇也——
　　　　（唱）大小三軍聽號令，
　　　　　　　君臨天下建奇功。
　　　　　　　點兵擂鼓齊震動，
　　　　　　　隨朕殺——殺殺殺殺殺殺殺，殺一個乾乾淨淨、
　　　　　　　寸草不生、普天同慶滿江紅！

端木格： 這聲音——可不是——？（大喊）陛下！

邠赫拉： （置若罔聞，仍然看著石頭）那些傢伙，以前奉承朕。
　　　　朕說什麼就是什麼，乖得很哪。但那一回風雨不聽命令，
　　　　吹得朕渾身打顫，雷電也響個不停，老身就看穿他們了。
　　　　這群狗腿的話根本不算數。

端木格： （再次大喊）陛下！

邠赫拉： 來來來，你過來，過來（取出一片樹葉，遞過去）代朕

宣讀這〈討叛逆檄〉。

端木格：陛下，老臣看不見哪。

邠赫拉：（仍拿著樹葉，不耐煩）快宣讀啊。

端木格：恕老臣不能用眼眶來讀啊。

邠赫拉：哦，（轉頭打量端木格）你沒眼珠，又沒元寶，哈哈！
　　　　那你怎麼當月老？（帶著哭音）端木格的私生子都比朕
　　　　的女兒孝順啊！（嚴厲）你的紅繩頭，還是亂牽的好。
　　　　（左顧右盼）噓，你看到豺狼當道了麼？

端木格：老臣感受到了。

邠赫拉：這就是了。雙眼看不清，就用兩耳看分明吧。你瞧見賤
　　　　狗榮登大寶了麼？賤狗若是當道，你就得服從牠。權威
　　　　就是這麼一回事。

端木格：（以衣袖拭淚）陛下！

邠赫拉：（看看端木格）哭得好！朕恕你無罪。我們哭著出生，
　　　　只因為這裡多的是傻瓜，都在蝸牛角上爭名奪利。別哭
　　　　了，你若歡喜，老身的眼珠大可相贈。

端木格：天哪！

邠赫拉：（絕望）反正老身──（低聲）有眼也無用……

　　　　（端木加復上）

端木加：（看到邠赫拉）可憐哪，陛下瘋了！
　　　　（司徒德原貌上，遠遠望見邠赫拉）

司徒德：（回頭呼喊）王后，陛下在此！

都　維：（內唱，上）急匆匆返軒轅痛心疾首，

尋陛下晝夜忙在此羈留。

斜陽外景依然故人非舊，

容顏改憔悴損邊幅不修。

（奔向邲赫拉，下跪，白）陛下啊——

（續唱）似這般狼狽樣前所未有，

誓出師絕不能善罷干休。

邲赫拉：（不可置信）你⋯⋯你是王母娘娘麼？朕是否已然駕崩？（下跪，司徒德忙扶起）

都　維：（淚下）女兒來遲了，皇娘恕罪。

（邲赫拉欲走）

都　維：（起身拉住邲）蒼天啊！求求您治好她吧。這是個被逼瘋的母親啊。即使是我仇家的惡犬，在那種風雨夜，本宮也會讓牠留在火爐邊。姐姐們何其忍心！

邲赫拉：朕早已安息，你們不該吵醒我。朕在哪裡？

都　維：（悲慟）皇娘、皇娘！您看看我，（下跪）我是維兒，您的維兒啊！

邲赫拉：啊，不要嘲笑老身，老身不過是個愚昧昏瞶的老太婆！老身糊塗了。不要哭泣。（仔細端詳）果真是⋯⋯維兒？（扶起）

都　維：（拭淚）是，正是。

邲赫拉：（羞愧低頭）朕——對不住你！沒有恩賜給你啊！

都　維：皇娘平安，就是最大的恩賜。

邲赫拉：朕是在赫連國麼？

都　維：不，您在軒轅境內。女兒此番興師問罪，毫無侵犯軒轅

之意，不過是為皇娘討還公道罷了。

邬赫拉：唉，朕已垂垂老矣，這公道麼——

　　　　（唱）公道二字何曾有？

　　　　　　　人謀不臧徒遭憂。

　　　　　　　分疆之日堪回首？

　　　　　　　理應怨懟如寇讎。

　　　　　　　滿腹愧疚難出口，

　　　　　　　老身懵懂萬事休。

都　維：皇娘啊——

　　　　（唱）公道自在人心有，

　　　　　　　盡孝毋須問緣由。

　　　　　　　皇娘此言休出口，

　　　　　　　分疆之事早拋丟。

　　　　　　　另尋良醫回春手，

　　　　　　　事陛下、享天倫、笑顏開，從此無慮亦無憂。

　　　　（擁抱邬赫拉，二人對泣）

司徒德：（下跪）臣司徒德叩見陛下。

　　　　（邬赫拉茫然）

都　維：司徒大人請起，陛下心智尚未完全恢復。

　　　　（端木格由端木加攙扶至前）

端木格：老臣叩見王后。（欲下跪）

都　維：（伸手扶住）大人忠心護主，慘遭荼毒，司徒大人皆已
　　　　詳告，還請受本后一拜。

端木格：（欠身亦拜）不敢，老臣但盡本分。這是小兒端木加。

　　　（端木加上前施禮）

都　維：免。令郎之冤，本后盡知，日後定會妥善處置。

端木格、端木加：謝王后。

司徒德：王后，軒轅大軍已然集結，還請速返營區，共商大計。

都　維：大人言之有理。（攙扶邠赫拉）皇娘，來吧。

　　　（眾下）

　　　（切光）

第九場　國殤

（曠野）

（兩軍交戰，群舞隊形，聲光變化）

【幕後伴唱】：旌旗蔽空戰鼓響，

凌陣車轂交錯忙。

短兵相接銳難擋，

奮勇爭先士氣昂。

敵眾我寡聲悲壯，

（端木蒙上）

端木蒙：來人哪！戰俘押入大牢。

（侍衛押解邠赫拉、都維、優丹及若干赫連軍士上）

【幕後續唱】：敗者為寇勝者王。

都　維：皇娘恕罪，女兒無能！

邠赫拉：不妨。（搖搖手）現在，就只有娘和你——

（唱）歲月靜好從此隱，

相依相伴度晨昏。

閒看彩蝶穿花陣，

家常無事笑語親。

（兩軍繼續無聲廝殺，赫連漸敗）

都　維：（動容，續唱）低聲傾訴小秘密，

　　　　　　　承歡惟有一片心。

　　　（兩軍繼續無聲廝殺，軒轅大勝）

邙赫拉：（拍拍都維，續唱）世道了然不須問，

　　　　　　　　　　　繁華落盡見真淳。

端木蒙：押下去。

　　　（侍衛押解邙赫拉、都維、優丹及若干赫連軍士下）

　　　侍衛長！

侍衛長：屬下在。

端木蒙：傳大公主口諭：入大牢後，立即絞殺赫連王后，不得有誤。

侍衛長：遵命。（下）

　　　（南宮奧、都緒、都紹、眾侍衛上）

南宮奧：端木將軍，蒼天保佑，你作戰英勇，力克敵軍，本宮將會論功行賞。而今戰俘安在？

端木蒙：兄弟已命人將戰俘全部押入大牢，聽候發落。

南宮奧：（不悅）兄弟？你是本宮的部屬，怎可與本宮兄弟相稱？

都　紹：那要看本宮高興怎麼賞賜他。端木將軍統領我軍，代行本宮一切職權，自然可以和您稱兄道弟。

都　緒：唷，別這麼親熱。他是憑藉自己的軍功步步高升，可不是你的冊封。

都　紹：哼，本宮當然有權冊封他。他可以和您們平起平坐。

南宮奧：哈哈，那他必須成為駙馬才行。

都　紹：（冷冷地）笑話常常成為預言。

都　緒：喝，住口！

都　紹：（捧腹）哎唷，好痛啊。

南宮奧：怎麼回事？

都　緒：（旁白）哼，不痛才怪！這可是巫師特製的毒藥呢。

都　紹：我——

南宮奧：二妹，你的臉色不好，回營歇息去吧。

　　　　來人，送二公主回去。

　　　　（一侍衛上，扶都紹下）

　　　　（侍衛丙上）

侍衛丙：稟駙馬，有一頭陀求見。

南宮奧：頭陀？——叫他過來。

　　　　（端木加喬裝成瘋頭陀，隨侍衛丙上，靠近南宮奧）

端木加：（低聲）駙馬爺，請別誤會，小人不是頭陀。借一步說話，小人有機密稟報。

　　　　（南宮奧一怔，立即作個手勢，二人趨前兩步）

南宮奧：你是何人？

端木加：小人端木加，暫時必須隱瞞身分，還請駙馬成全。

南宮奧：（打量端木加）果然是你！（低聲）有何機密？

端木加：駙馬看信便知。

　　　　（呈信，南宮奧讀信）

都　緒：阿蒙，怎麼還沒動手？

端木蒙：此話怎講？請公主明示。

都　緒：（瞪視端木蒙）怎麼？你沒收到信麼？

　　　　（都緒與端木蒙低聲交談；南宮奧讀信，愈發惱怒）

南宮奧：（壓抑，咬牙切齒）大膽賤人，竟妄想勾結端木蒙謀害

　　　　本宮？

端木加：駙馬，家父日前不幸亡故，臨終之前，交代小人務必清
　　　　理門戶。請恩准小人和這不肖阿蒙比劍，親手報仇。

南宮奧：這——好吧。

　　　　（南宮奧、端木加返回原處）

　　　　（嚴肅）本宮接獲密報，端木蒙有意謀反。

都　緒：（一驚）駙馬胡說些什麼？

端木蒙：絕無此事。駙馬有何憑證？

南宮奧：證據確鑿，不得抵賴。公主，（亮信）罪證在此！

　　　　（都緒欲奪信）

南宮奧：（阻攔）豈容你湮滅證據！

都　緒：哼！本宮是公主，你能奈我何？（拂袖下）

南宮奧：來人，好好看住她！

　　　　（侍衛丙承應，下）

端木蒙：公主有何計謀，末將全然不知，尚請駙馬明察。

南宮奧：不必多言。本應立即處斬你，但蒼天自有公道的安排。
　　　　現在，本宮宣布端木蒙與密報者（指端木加）比劍。
　　　　（向端木蒙）邪不勝正，你就用寶劍來證明自己的清白
　　　　吧。

端木蒙：笑話！竟要我跟一個瘋頭陀比劍？

端木加：吾非瘋頭陀，吾乃正義之化身。

南宮奧：（舉劍）比劍開始。

端木加：看劍！

　　　　（端木加、端木蒙比劍數回合）

　　　　（端木蒙中劍倒地）

端木蒙：（聲音微弱）你……你的劍術……你是何人？

端木加： 天理昭彰，（恢復原貌）吾乃端木加，被你誣陷之兄長。

端木蒙： 啊，竟然是你！

　　　　（眾人大驚）

　　　　（侍衛丙衝上）

侍衛丙： 稟駙馬，大事不好！兩位公主都——歸天了！

南宮奧：（大驚）什麼？

侍衛丙： 大公主服毒自盡，二公主也被她下了毒。

端木蒙：（苦笑）哈，這回蒼天安排咱仨個同時成親了。

南宮奧： 報應真是歷歷不爽啊。

　　　　（司徒德蹣跚上）

司徒德： 駙馬，老臣即將遠行，特來向陛下辭行。陛下不在此處
　　　　麼？

南宮奧： 竟忘了這樁大事！來人，去大牢釋放陛下和赫連王后，
　　　　請他們過來。

端木蒙：「人之將死，其言也善」——快去，因為大公主已下令
　　　　處死赫連王后。

南宮奧： 可惡！（向侍衛）快去！快馬加鞭！

　　　　（一侍衛承應，下）

端木蒙： 唉，枉費心機，到頭來不過……（斷氣）

端木加： 一場空。

南宮奧：（揮手）拖下去。

　　　　（一侍衛承應，拖下）

列位，社稷不幸，百廢待舉。本宮有意退位，歸政於女皇。但當務之急，尚須借重各位長才，共同興復家邦。（向端木加）端木大人，請承襲令尊之位，協助本宮安撫百姓。

端木加：是，微臣定當盡力。

（二侍衛抬都維上，邠赫拉、優丹隨上）

邠赫拉：維兒、維兒！你怎麼不說話了？

優　丹：大嬸，節哀啊，人死不能復生。

邠赫拉：蒼天哪──

（唱）撲簌簌悲從中來椎心泣，

　　　聲聲喚喚不回朕的小嬌兒！

　　　思往事彷彿溫柔亭亭立，

　　　凜凜然松柏後凋歲寒姿；

　　　凝神看冷若冰霜失生氣，

　　　徒留下、老娘親、悔恨綿綿無絕期。

（悲泣，白）維兒啊──

（續唱）問蒼天骨肉相殘何時已？

　　　煮豆怎忍燃豆萁？

　　　問蒼天五倫莫非風雅體？

　　　治國容廢萬世基？

　　　問蒼天人間公義何處覓？

　　　善惡報應豈無稽？

　　　問蒼天因緣了斷生與死？

　　　　　黃粱一夢惟存疑！

　　　　　既知人情薄如紙，

　　　　　當面奉承暗裡譏，

　　　　　不堪留戀塵俗事，

　　　　　另尋天地無所羈。

　　（白）維兒、維兒，等等娘啊！（踉蹌倒地而亡）

　　（眾人大驚，侍衞丙上前查看）

侍衞丙：稟駙馬，陛下她——駕崩了！

南宮奧：（仰天）唉，軒轅不幸，舉國哀悼！

　　　　　（下跪，眾皆跪）

　　　　　（下接〈尾聲〉）

尾　聲

（優丹持酒杯上前）

優　丹：（神情莊重，唱）一念之差鐘鼎毀，

蒼天戲弄不勝悲。

萬物有靈傷其類，

特來問取酒一杯。

（灑酒於地，以示祭奠）

（向觀眾，續唱）落花無言隨流水，

多少青史盡成灰。

諸君觀戲有體會，

散場繼續說——是——非。

（切光）

劇　終

設計圖稿
(Illustrations of
Costume and Stage Designs)

1-1. 邠赫拉（Empress）

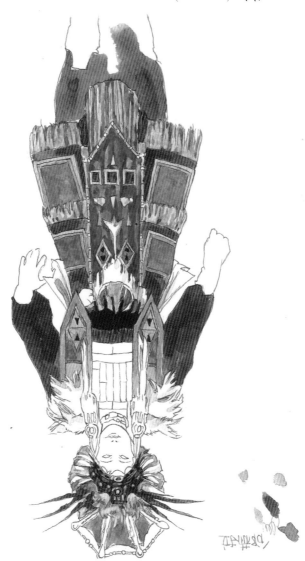

1-3. 邠赫拉（Empress）

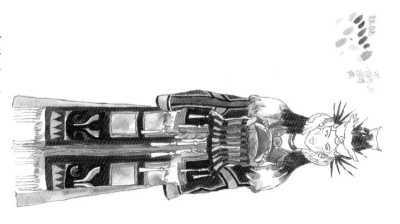

2. 郁稽（Xu）

3. 郁紹（Shao）

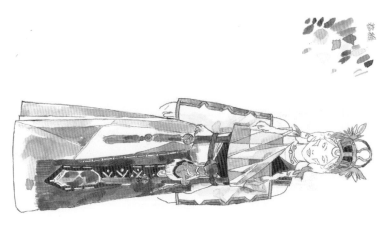

郁維

4-1. 郁維（Wei）

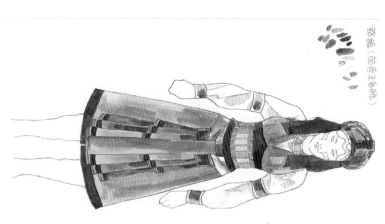

郁維（英雄王名郁維）

4-2. 郁維（Wei）

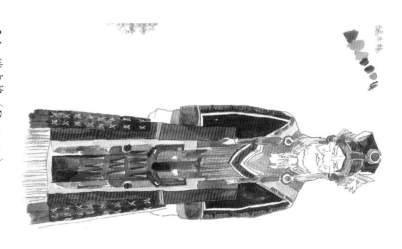

5-1. 端木格（Duanmu）

5-2. 端木格（Duanmu）

6-1. 端木加 (A-Jia)

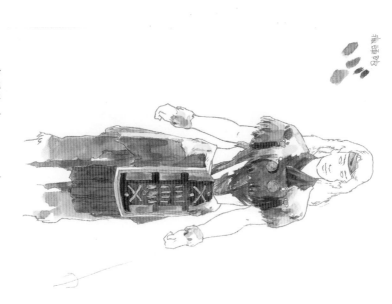

6-2. 瘋頭陀 (mad monk)

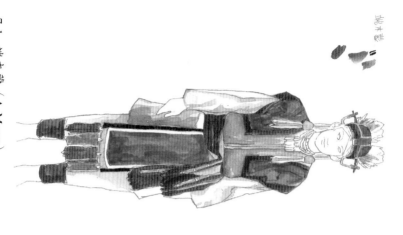

7-1. 端木豪 (A-Meng)

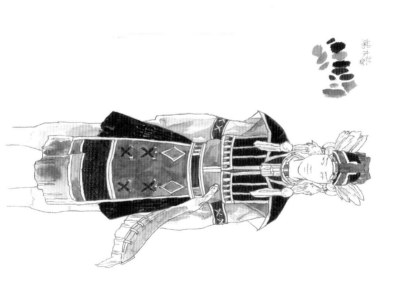

7-2. 端木豪 (A-Meng)

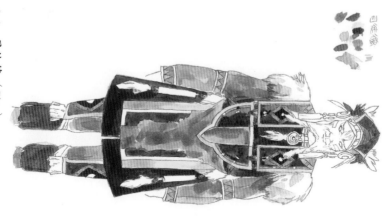

8-1. 司徒德 (Situ)

8-2. 公孫凱 (Gongsun)

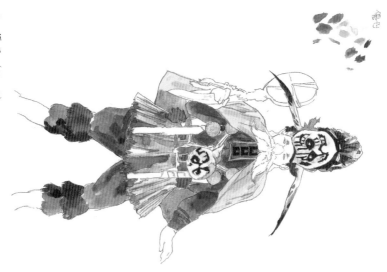

9. 優丹（Fool）

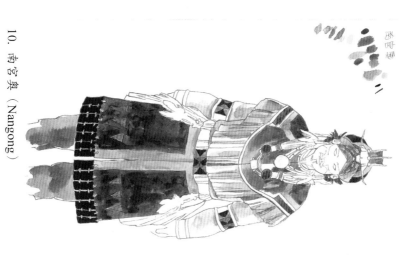

10. 南宮奧（Nangong）

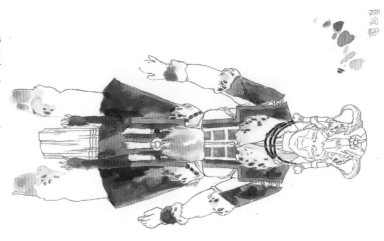

11. 夏侯康 (Xiahou)

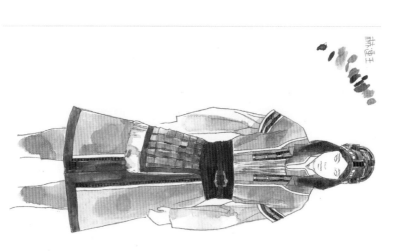

12. 赫連王 (Helian)

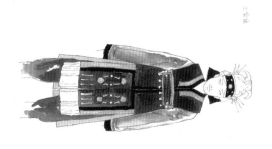

13. 上官達（Shangguan）

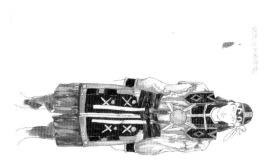

14. 郇赫拉系統侍衛
（Guard under the Empress）

15. 赫連王系統侍衛
（Guard under Helian）

舞台一